PAWADA

A Novel

PAWADA

A Novel

Wimaladasa Samarasinghe

Translation
Apsara Karunaratna
Wimaladasa Samarasinghe

&

STERLING PUBLISHERS (P) LTD.
Regd. Office: A1/256 Safdarjung Enclave,
New Delhi-110029. Cin: U22110DL1964PTC211907
Phone: +91 82877 98380
e-mail: mail@sterlingpublishers.in
www.sterlingpublishers.in

Co-Published in Sri Lanka by
PAHAN PUBLICATIONS
No. 717/1 Maradana Road
Colombo 10, Sri Lanka.
Telephone No: 011-5852714
pahanpublications@gmail.com

PAWADA: A Novel
© 2020, Wimaladasa Samarasinghe
ISBN 978-93-86245-67-0

All rights are reserved.
No part of this publication may be reproduced, stored in a retrieval system or transmitted, in any form or by any means, mechanical, photocopying, recording or otherwise, without prior written permission of the original publisher.

Printed in India

Printed and Published by Sterling Publishers Pvt. Ltd.,
Plot No. 13, Ecotech-III, Greater Noida - 201306,
Uttar Pradesh, India

1

"*Ataka naataka Wepata Sungam-Kodi Alappan-Aam Baam buusi Kole-Mung Aragan Yoda Kole…*" while tapping on to the hands stretched downside on the bench in a row, Piyasena raised his head before tapping on to the next hand which was Addin's.

"Take away your hands. We will not take you for the game," shouted Piyasena.

"Hey, take your hands away," Sumathipala too joined in. All gave Addin a disgusted look. Both Piyasena and Sumathipala were heftier than Addin.

Addin took his hands away while pinching Piyasena's shoulder.

"Ouch!" said Piyasena and gave a hard blow on Addin's head.

Addin too didn't retreat and treated Piyasena with a hard blow on his head.

Others in the game got back and there ended the game.

"*Radawa*," called out Piyasena.

"Wild ass," Addin reacted.

"*Rada* dog," Piyasena shouted at him and everyone followed him.

When one scolded Addin mentioning his caste he used to get angry. He took his stone slate lying on the bench and hit Piyasena with it.

'Everything is finished,' thought Addin. Everyone dispersed. Piyasena started to cry loudly. The teacher in the adjoining class came to see what had happened. 'This is going to be a disaster, they will have an inquiry for this, and take me to the principal sir for punishment', thought Addin as fear was creeping into him.

He collected the broken pieces of the slate and held his books tight, close to his bosom and ran out of the class room to the road, and then ran along the road without looking back. He turned to look back after running a long way on the road.

On his way to home he saw someone fishing with a fishing rod in the river, flowing just adjoining the road, from the grove of Beli. Addin placed the broken stone slate and his books beside the grove and climbed a branch of the Beli tree. Then he started to watch the man fishing, sitting on the branch in the Beli grove. 'This is very interesting', he thought.

Sunrays were appearing hard in the cloudless sky.

Addin stepped down from the Beli tree when he heard the noise of the children returning home after school. He came out of the Beli grove and joined them.

"Hey... Addin you'll be punished tomorrow. We will tell that you ran away from school and were hiding here," one of Addin's schoolmates warned him.

Addin was in Grade Two at that time. He was Batto's younger son. Some called 'Batto Vidane' as 'Batto maama' and some called him 'Vidane' or 'Batto'. The elderly males of their caste were called as Hene mama by the villagers. The elderly men and women of Batto's caste were generally known as Vidane and 'Redi Nenda,' respectively. Therefore Addin's mother was known as 'Redi Nenda' or just 'Nenda'. Though they were called 'Maama', the uncle, and 'Nenda', the aunt, the terms were by no means meant to show their relationship as relatives. Those were the special terms used for a washerman and washerwoman.

Batto's house was located closer to the river. Their house was known as the *'Rada Gedara'*, the house of the washers, among the villagers. Batto's house was located about seven or eight metres away from the road. Beyond the road there was a narrow belt of land with several trees. Some of those trees were bent towards the river. In between those trees and the road was a grove of Areca nut trees.

In the afternoon that day Addin was looking at the river water leaning against an Areca nut tree. Suddenly, he saw Piyasena coming with someone towards his house. They came down the road and stopped at the stile in front of Batto's house. The other person accompanying Piyasena was his father. Piyasena's father crossed over the stile and stopped in Battos's courtyard and spoke to him aggressively.

"Batto, look here!"

Batto, who was ironing clothes in the house, came out when he heard the noise.

"Where is your little one? He has hit my son with his slate. Our children are not there to be beaten by the Radawas. You are going to lose your house," shouted Piyasena's father who was known as Dingi Mahattaya among the villagers. He scolded Batto as much as he could and Batto endured all that with great difficulty. What else could he do other than listening to him? "Honourable sir, I'll punish my son," Batto pleaded to Dingi Mahattaya. Addin remained still; leaning against the Areca nut tree. No one could see him from their house. Piyasena's face was all swollen from the blow he had received from Addin in the school.

"Boy! Come here," Batto called Addin in a severe tone after Piyasena and his father left. He broke a stem of a tree and started hitting him continuously without uttering a word. Addin had nothing else to do other than to cry loudly. As Addin's mother was away from home in the evening taking the clothes to the houses in the village, no one came to his rescue. Addin's sister Babi was only watching the way her father was hitting her brother.

The next day Addin went to school not for his own liking but on the persuasion of Batto and Redi Nenda. Addin was trying his best to avoid going to school and stay at home. But, he had to go to school with his father. Batto used to wear a white sarong that was given to be washed by a villager. He did not wear anything to cover his upper body, nor were they in the habit of wearing anything to cover their upper body. Batto was walking in front with a shawl around his neck that had been given to him to be washed. Addin was walking behind him like a slow rat. Broken slate and the book were in Addin's right hand. Addin realised that the initial urge Batto had to accompany him to school had disappeared noticing the condescension as his walk started to slow down. Children were playing all over the school premises, and making a lot of noise.

Batto Vidane and Addin stopped at the room of the principal. Batto entered the room reluctantly; Addin too followed him and leaned against the wall. As soon as Batto saw the principal sir sitting on a big chair, the shawl on his shoulder fell on his hand. He took it and wrapped it around his waist.

Batto spoke in a smattering tone.

"Sir, my boy has committed a blunder yesterday. I came here to tell you about it," Batto said with difficulty.

"Yes, yes, I got to know that he ran away from the school," said the headmaster in an inconsiderate heavy tone.

"The boy was trying to miss school, but I decided to bring him to you," Vidane spoke in a pleading tone.

"We will hear the case and punish the culprits; you may go home," said the headmaster. "You can go to the class," he said and sent Addin to his class.

"Ok Sir," said Batto and turned back to go home.

After Batto Vidane left for home, Addin went to his class shivering like a fish out of water, thinking about the punishment he was going to get at any moment.

After Batto left the school, the headmaster came to Addin's class. He took Addin to his room. The pain he suffered from the five strokes of cane on his right palm was unforgettable.

2

Batto comes from a washer family in Athuraliya village. Batto's father too lived in the same village. Even his grandfather lived in the Athuraliya village. Batto believed that his children and grandchildren would continue to live in the same village. And he also believed that people of his generation should live in the same village. Batto had a withered body, a bony face, and blackish teeth due to betel chewing. His mien was of an exerted rough life, full of difficulties.

The closest city to the Athuraliya village was Matara, which was twelve miles away. Nilwala River bordered the village from one side and also flowed through the village.

Though Nilwala River was a common disaster to the whole village, Batto and his family's survival was dependent on the river. Nilwala River overflowed at least twice or thrice a year. The flood used to wash away the whole village. Therefore, for people in the village floods, droughts, winds, rains were all common occurrences and they were a part of their lives. They knew that the river would overflow in May and December every year.

Athuraliya was a small village that consisted of seven or eight small islands surrounded by paddy fields. Many in the village had small plots of land. Many families had constructed small wattle houses on those lands, while several in the village were undergoing hardships. There were only about seven or eight well-to-do families in the entire village. Many of the large lands belonged to those rich families.

Even Batto's house with the land and the adjoining coconut estate belonged to Vidane Mahattaya. He was among one of the richest men in the village.

The road from Matara to Athuraliya ran parallel to the river and it went across the river at Kadduwa. There was a timber bridge across the river at Kadduwa. One bus operated from Matara to Kadduwa but it could not cross the river, so there was no bus service for those two miles from Kadduwa to Athuraliya. Even the one bus that ran on that route was in a state of disrepair and therefore could travel only about one or two trips. Thus people used to travel that distance by foot. People walked the distance of about two kilometres from Kadduwa to Athuraliya and other paths that led to the interior of the village.

There was a small dispensary run by the government for the villagers to get medicine free of charge. A doctor visited the dispensary twice a week. He had some white tablets and a pink liquid to prescribe for fever and cold. One had to go there early morning and first obtain a ticket from the caretaker of the dispensary to consult the doctor and then to get the medicine.

Patients in the queue were all scared of the caretaker. He was the one who directed the patients one by one to the doctor. The doctor in the room checked patients with his stethescope and the villagers in Athuraliya got cured by his medicines.

When those medicines did not work on them, they used to go to the Matara General Hospital.

Batto once went to the Matara General Hospital when Addin was eleven years old to get treatment for polio. He had to carry Addin on the shoulder for about two kilometres up to Kadduwa. The doctor of the Kadduwa dispensary told them to take him immediately to the Matara general hospital as Addin's condition was bad. Addin was admitted to the hospital and Batto returned home the very same night. Addin recovered after six days and he was discharged from the hospital. Out of those six days, Batto's family could only go to see Addin for three days.

"Don't let this child exert himself a lot for another three to four months. Don't let him run here and there. You would have to take care of him. Otherwise, this child would be crippled, said the doctor to Batto when Addin was discharged from the hospital. Batto took off the handkerchief on his shoulder to his left hand and said "ok sir," bending his head in obeisance to the doctor.

Batto carried Addin on his shoulder from the hospital to the bus stand. He never felt Addin's weight.

"There's lot of time for the next bus," he heard someone mention at the bus-stand. Addin had to sit on a boundary wall for a long time until the bus arrived. Batto was sitting next to him impatiently.

Batto got off from the Bus from Kadduwa, released a long breath, and took Addin onto his shoulder again. He walked silently for about two kilometers up to his home on a path that was full of gravel. He only gave a short reply to something asked by Addin. The road which was in a state of disrepair made him more tired and he put down Addin twice or thrice to rest for a few minutes.

"The boy escaped this time too," said Batto and put him down on the verandah. Batto was feeling relaxed. Redi Nenda heard his voice and came towards them.

"The boy is lucky," said Redi Nenda.

"The doctor told us to take good care of him," replied Batto.

"Hey, boy, did you hear? You should not go out to play," said Redi Nenda to Addin.

Just as Batto Vidane, Redi Nenda too was used to endure so many hardships. Though, she spoke a lot with her kids, she never spoke much with her husband. Both of them only believed that everyone in the family must endure any hardship without questioning. All of them including the children had become used to enduring any threat whatsoever caused by droughts, rains, winds, animals, ill-treatment by others and considered such things natural.

3

"Hewa Radage Addin," it was how his name was called out by the headmaster of the school. Later on he read out his name as H.R. Addin.

Other boys in Addin's class had names such as Piyasena, Sumathipala, Siripala, Sirisena. They were either Dasas, Palas, or Senas. Only two or three had names such as Addin or Martin, and such names were considered inferior. Therefore, some called him "Adding" and others called him "Addin."

Addin's name was given to him by the village headman, the *Ralahami*. When Batto went to *Ralahami* to register his birth, he was asked about the name given to the boy.

"Batto, what's the name of the boy?" asked the *Ralahami*.

"Sir, isn't it good to call him Piyasena?" asked Batto.

Though, 'Piyasena' was the name given by Batto, after getting the birth certificate his name had been changed to Addin. That's how Addin got his name. *Ralahami* did not allow him to get a good name for Addin.

Addin used to wear a dress called *Jangiya* to the school. That was a dress locally prepared as a single unit having three openings on top to put head and two arms and another two openings down to put two legs.

Redi Nenda, the washer woman, did not sew *Jangiyas* for him, because they had enough of *Jangiyas* from the clothes that were given to them for washing that belonged to children of his age. When *Jangiyas* were brought for washing Addin could wear it for about a week. Not only Addin, but his sister and his brother too had the opportunity to wear some of the clothes belonging to others. Therefore, they went to school dressed in dirty clothes that were given to be washed by the villagers. Sometimes, they even went to Matara to buy medicine in the same dirty clothes. They were not dirty for them.

The washed clothes were distributed to the houses in the village by the washer woman. Addin also accompanied Redi Nenda when she visited houses. "I cannot go from door to door carrying clothes," replied Samy when he was asked to accompany her too. Redi Nenda hung the bundle of clothes on her shoulder bending a little forward in an experienced manner. It was a talent she had inherited from her ancestry. She used to wrap the washed clothes in a large piece of cloth and tie a knot bringing the four corners of the cloth together and would go door to door and bring back dirty clothes in the same manner tied in the cloth.

Redi Nenda used to enter a house from the rear door instead the front. That too was a common practice she inherited from her ancestry. They were not allowed to enter into any house of a higher caste from the front door because they belonged to the Rada caste. Seeing Redi Nenda entering the house, an elderly woman would arrange a low chair for her to sit. There are small chairs in almost every house in the village. None from Batto's family could sit on a high chair. The villagers too would never offer them high chairs to sit. Addin was leaning against his mother's body.

Women in the village would learn new stories about their neighbours from Redi Nenda. "Any news around the boutique, Nende?" Hamine would ask. So Redi Nenda would relate new stories about the villagers with Hamine.

"Is it true that your boy wears our clothes given for washing?" asked Hamine.

"Oh! No Hamine," pleaded Redi Nenda.

"If your boy wears our clothes hereafter I will stop giving you clothes," warned Hamine.

Though she promised never to do it, it was difficult for Redi Nenda's family to refrain themselves from wearing dirty clothes. Because they didn't have sufficient clothes to wear.

Though they washed a lot of clothes they would only get some rice sufficient for two seasons and some money that they were given after the New Year, as labour charges. After the paddy harvest in the village, Batto Vidane would take a gunny sack with him and go to the houses to collect paddy given to him by the villagers. His family survived with that paddy throughout the year. Other than that they did not receive any money as wage. Though the paddy given to them used to be sufficient earlier, later on it became insufficient for the whole family. With the passage of time, villagers stopped giving them paddy for their service and instead started giving a bit of money.

They used to visit their customers' houses for the New Year meal. The first visit was made to the Henegedara Mudalali's house. They belived that paying their first visit to the Mudalali's for the New Year and receiving money from him brought good luck. Therefore, Batto Vidane, Redi Nenda, Addin, Samy and Babi visited Mudalali's place for the New Year. All in the village called him 'Henegedara Mudalali' but Batto's family added the suffix 'Mahattaya' or Sir at the end of every name; Mudalali too was called 'Mudalali Mahattaya' by them.

Redi Nenda and Vidane sat on the two small chairs provided by Mudalali's wife while Addin, Babi, and Samy stood leaning against the wall. Mudalali's wife got a glass of water for Redi Nenda but did not offer water to Addin and his siblings as they were kids. Then she placed plates of milk rice and fried sprats on their hands. The cups and plates that were used to offer them food were kept separately in their house and they did not use the plates to partake meals. Many plates that were used to offer food to Batto Vidane's family were partly broken, discolored and old ones. After finishing the plate of milk rice with fried sprats, they were given water in a partly broken cup. They were given sweets such as *Keum, kokis* and some other sweets from some houses.

Then the Mudalali gave them money. He gave two rupees note each wrapped in a betel leaf to Vidane and Redi Nenda, while Addin, Babi, and Samy were given ten cents each. Then, Hamine gave one rupee each to Vidane and Redi Nenda followed by her daughter who gave Vidane and Redi Nenda one rupee each. They gave them this money as their annual wage for washing their clothes throughout the year. Batto's family visited all the houses of the village for the New Year that sought their services. For some houses Redi Nenda accompanied Babi; if not, she would go with Addin. They preferred to eat milk rice with fried sprats or onions and thus the children loved to go with their mother to enjoy the New Year tidbits given by the villagers. They did not get two rupees from each house, some gave them one rupee or fifty cents, but that too was a large amount for them.

4

In the *Veralu* season, the tree bore lots of fruits. Children went to the school early in the morning to pick the *Veralu* fruit from under the tree. On such days Addin went to the school earlier than others and used to pick a lap full of *Veralu*. When he would collect a lot of *Veralu*, others in the class used to become friendly with Addin and on such days all in the class wanted to be his friend.

"Please give me one!" and Addin would give one. "Please give me also one; you didn't give me a single," they would plead asking for *Veralu* and he would give each one a *Veralu*. But on the days when Piyasena or Sumathipala picked a lot of *Veralu*, they never gave Addin any, even if he would plead for one.

That day Addin went to school early in the morning, Piyasena came running to him and hit the lap full of *Veralu* that he had picked. They were scattered on the ground.

"Hey," Addin jumped at Piyasena. But it was useless. Piyasena picked up a few fruits of *Veralu* and ran away. Addin picked the rest and ran to the class. Piyasena did not even come closer to Addin the whole day.

There were long benches in Addin's class and one bench was sufficient for about eight kids. Piyasena was sitting at the edge of the bench. And Addin was sittng in the middle of the same bench. Addin was angry on Piyasena for snatching his *Veralu*. Addin was planning to take revenge.

Their teacher stepped out of the class to chew betel leaves with the teacher of the adjoining class.

There were two children sitting in between Piyasena and Addin. Addin murmured to Richard who was next to him, "Shall we push Piyasena from the bench?" and Richard agreed to the suggestion. But Richard was scared of Piyasena. Piyasena was hefty and Richard was smaller than him. Addin swiftly pushed the bench with the help of Richard.

Piyasena fell off to the ground with a bang. Piyasena got up and started to beat up Addin. Hearing the noise their teacher came to the class.

"What is going on?"

"Piyasena hit me," replied Addin with tears.

"Teacher, Addin pushed me from the bench," said Piyasena in a crying tone.

"Teacher, Addin pushed Piyasena from the bench," said all the children in unison.

"Come here," the teacher called Addin angrily in front of the class.

"Give me your hand," and she caned Addin's palm several times until it hurt.

"You should know who you are," said the teacher while punishing him.

5

"Children, now you can go to the garden and those who couldn't add fertiliser to their plots can go find cow dung for the vegetable beds," said the teacher loudly to her students and all the children got up from their seats and left the class. Addin was also among them.

Each one of them left for their respective vegetable beds and some went to fetch their *mamoty* and spades. Others went to collect cow dung onto an areca leaf as it's to easier to drag it on the ground.

There were only three areca leaves. There were eight children assigned to bring cow dung. Addin was also among the crowd. Those without an areca leaf joined with others who had leaves. Addin too joined Richard and collected cow dung.

There was ample cow dung in the rubber estate in the land adjoining the school. All in the class used to go there to collect cow dung. The rubber estate was stretched across a vast area. There was a jungle of berries beoynd the rubber estate. Anyone who went to collect cow dung, used to go to the berry forest and it was full of many other fruits. Whenever they used to visit the rubber estate they were able to collect a lot of fascinating things. Rubber seeds, rubber kernel, outer cover of rubber seeds were their ideal toys and playmates.

They returned to their classes with four or five rubber seeds with them. During the interval, when all the children left the class they secretly used to keep rubber seeds under the legs of the benches. When the children return to the class sat on the bench, the seeds burst with a noise.

"There, he broke the bench," others would shout and laugh at it.

"Hey, who placed rubber seeds under my bench?" someone might ask.

"We don't know," was the reply of another.

They ususally spent about two or three hours in the rubber estate collecting cow dung. Their delay was not at all a problem to the teachers.

All the teachers would gather in one place during the interval and drink tea while chatting. There were only four female teachers and three male teachers including the headmaster for the whole school. The headmaster stayed at the school premises, and so would go home to have tea.

Even though, the children went far to collect cow dung, they would return to school by the interval time. Interval was the best time Addin preferred in the time table. Children were given buns during the interval. The monitor used to bring buns in a basin. Addin loved the sight of yellow buns sprinkled with sugar.

On certain days some children did not eat the buns and used to give it to their friends or to whosoever wanted to eat them. Such days were lucky days for Addin. Though, Addin ate others' buns, the others in the class never asked for his bun. Addin too never offered his bun to anyone in the class.

"Today was a lucky day. I had two buns," Addin used to tell Babi on some days.

6

They piled up the dirty clothes collected from houses for days in a corner of their house. The dirty clothes at times emitted an unbearable smell. But the smell was familiar for the folks in Batto's house. When a large number of clothes were collected, Batto made a mark on the clothes from a dye, made out of almond seeds. Each house was given one unique sign. If the mark was missing, the clothes were more likely to get mixed. The mark was a dot, two dots, a line and a dot, a dot above the line or below the line and a dot on either side of the line. Batto marked each cloth in an invisible spot on the dress.

Wellawa or *Wella-heliya* that was used to boil dirty clothes in steam was prepared by Redi Nenda. Only a person, who was conversant with the art of preparing it, could do it well and it was difficult for another person to do it. Babi was still too small to prepare the *Wellawa*. It was a huge mud pot with water put on a hearth and clothes that are washed and squeezed should be piled up on the neck of the pot. Babi was assigned to put firewood into the hearth of the *Wellawa* and continue to put fire until the water in the pot boils.

"Babi, you look after the hearth to put fire," told Redi Nenda from the verendah. Babi put fire in to the hearth several times.

Redi Nenda got up early and cleared up the *Wellawa* early in the morning, the following day. Then she tied up the clothes boiled in *Wellawa* into two big bundles. By the time she finished clearing *Wellawa* and preparing two bundles, Babi prepared tea for them. They put sugar onto their palms and drank down the cup of plain tea.

Batto carried the biggest bundle of clothes on his shoulder and Redi Nenda took the other one. On certain days Addin too accompanied them. Though it was easy for Addin to carry the heavy bundle, Redi Nenda carried the bundle with much difficulty. She walked leaning forward from the weight of the bundle of clothes.

They passed the stile at the end of the courtyard and crossed the tar road and then walked on a footpath across the grove and reached the ferry. The ferry where they used to wash clothes earlier was located in front of their house. But, as the river bank was eroded they had to change the ferry.

They went to the ferry early in the morning. No one was there at the ferry when they came. And they would start slapping clothes soaked in the river water one by one against the stone. There was a special stone at the ferry which they used for slapping clothes. The stone had become whitish due to soap and soda. Sometimes Addin also went there and waited on the bank while his parents washed clothes. He loved to watch them washing clothes. They were slapping clothes according to a rhythm taking turns. The sound of slapping of clothes echoed around the river. At times, they would exchange clothes from one hand to the other and therefore, slapping clothes was an exciting thing for Addin to watch.

It was an open place surrounded by groves and the river water was clear and flowed down slowly. They slapped each cloth on the stone and soaked it again in the water to wash and then drained the water in it. Then they threw it on to the wider cloth spread on the river bank.

Batto as well as Redi Nenda never got exhausted of washing clothes. Therefore, they washed clothes continuously for few hours. They stopped it only when they wanted to chew betel or have their breakfast.

Babi prepared something for breakfast at home until Batto Vidane and Redi Nenda washed clothes at the ferry. Then she brought rice for their breakfast to the ferry.

"*Appochchi*, come and have your breakefast," Babi invited her father for breakfast, but he did not stop slapping clothes on the stone and they continued slapping for some more time as if they did not hear Babi`s invitation. Then she also went down to the river and joined them in slapping clothes.

"It is better if you have your breakfast," after sometime Redi Nenda told Batto. He then threw the cloth from his hand onto the heap of clothes on the river bank and washed his hands in the river water. Then he took a handful of water into his palm and rinsed his mouth in the flowing river. The water he poured out from his mouth was reddened with the betel leaves he was chewing. Then he took another mouthful of water and spit it back into the river and came out of the river.

Batto Vidane then took a tin plate with rice, squated on the ground and started eating.

While Batto was eating, Babi joined her mother in slapping clothes. But she was unable to do the task as professionally as her mother and father.

After Batto finished eating, Redi Nenda went out of the river to eat her food after serving rice to Addin and Babi.

"Addin, you also eat," Redi Nenda gave the plate of rice to Addin who was on the river bank.

After everyone finished eating Babi collected the plates and washed them in the river. "Addin, you go with your sister and bring us some betel leaves," commanded Batto Vidane to Addin when Babi was just about to leave for home.

It was Addin who used to bring plain tea to the river during the day time. Addin preferred to be at the ferry than the house.

They finished washing the clothes by noon, and then they tied them in a pile and took them back home. There were coir ropes tied between coconut trees at the back side of the house to dry clothes in the sunlight.

The clothes that were washed were dipped in blue or fabric whitener water by Redi Nenda before she put them to dry. Some of the clothes were hung on coir ropes, and the rest were left to dry on the grass in the hot sun. Water was sprayed on the clothes time to time to make them look whiter. Babi collected the dried clothes and brought them home in the evening. Addin too sometimes helped her to collect clothes. But Babi's brother Samy never helped her for anything.

Redi Nenda took the bundle of clothes ironed the previous day, from door to door in the afternoon. Babi would put ten to twelve coconut shells in to the stove in the kitchen to prepare coal for the iron. Then she would put some glowing coal in to the iron to get it heated. But it was Batto Vidane who ironed the clothes with the heated iron. He started ironing in the evening and continued till seven or eight o'clock in the night. Ironing clothes was not an easy task and not all are good at it, for it requires a lot of patience. As it started getting dark Redi Nenda returned home with a bundle of dirty clothes which were collected from houses and also got all the clothes that were left to dry. Then she started to prepare their dinner with the help of Babi.

7

Batto did not care much about educating his children. He considered school education as something undeserving for their family. Often when Redi Nenda pestered the kids to go to school, he tried to stop her. That's why Babi stopped schooling after grade two. "Schooling is not meant for us," Batto often said to his family.

Just as Samy, Addin too went to school with lack of interest. Sometimes, they went to school only three or four days a week. On other days, they would fabricate a reason to stay at home. But Redi Nenda did not like Addin staying back at home. She knew that Addin was good in his studies. But later on when Addin too was becoming lethargic to go to school, Redi Nenda did not want to persuade him.

"That is ok, you just stay at home, anyway only Babi is alone at home during day time," said Redi Nenda at last. Redi Nenda thought that if Addin stays back, Babi would not be left alone at home. She was happy that she could keep Addin at home while she was out of the house.

Batto Vidane too never commanded his children to go to school nor did he ask them to stop schooling.

However, he believed that educating their children would be of no use to them.

"Washing clothes has been our job for generations. We cannot give it up and start something else," said Batto. "How could you say so? We've got to educate them," said Redi Nenda.

Batto didn't give her any reply. But he believed that washing clothes of others in the village should be their job, and it's inappropriate for a person who's born to a family of the washer's caste to pursue education.

Though Addin did not like going to school, he loved to go to school at the end of the year when they were promoted from one grade to another. At that time the children got new uniforms and books when they went to a new class. Addin rarely got new clothes and books, yet he loved the feel of new books.

Addin withdrew his earnest request for new books when Redi Nenda said that they don't have money to buy new books for the new class. But Redi Nenda did not forget to ask for some used books of the previous year from a house of a student for Addin's use. For writing they used the unwritten pages of the old notebooks.

Redi Nenda knew that there was a boy from the upper grade in the house near the brook. She had taken his books for Addin's use last year too.

In the afternoon, Addin accompanied Redi Nenda when she went to distribute washed clothes and to collect dirty clothes. They went to the house by the brook. Redi Nenda entered the house from the rear entrance and kept the pile of clothes she was carrying on her shoulder, on the ground and sat on the small chair offered by Hamine. Addin leaned against his mother. Redi Nenda started the conversation. Hamine was checking the clothes brought by Redi Nenda.

"How did this blouse get torn Nende?" asked Hamine lifting one piece from the bundle.

"This's an old blouse Hamine, and it's already worn off," replied Redi Nenda.

"You have made this cloth discolored!" exclaimed Hamine.

"Hamine, you told me to boil this, didn't you? It's due to the boiling that it has got discolored," uttered Redi Nenda.

After Hamine finished checking her clothes, Redi Nenda started the topic of books. "Hamine, would you be able to give Punchi Mahattaya's old books to my boy?" asked Redi Nenda.

She referred 'Punchi Mahattaya' to the lady's son who studied in a higher grade in Addin's school. Batto's family used to address every small child who belonged to the higher caste families in the village as Punchi Mahattaya.

"What's the point in educating your children? They are not going to be school masters?" snorted Hamine.

"No, but they should at least be able to read something like a list of herbals given by Weda Mahattaya," answered Redi Nenda.

"If you had come yesterday, you would have got the books. But Poramba Hamine came yesterday and took two books with her for her kid. But I told her, you came last year as well and that you might come this time too", Redi Nenda had a feeling that Dole Gedara Hamine was lying to her.

"There are two more books of the boy, you may take those if you need," said Hamine.

Redi Nenda left that house with those two books. For Addin, it was like conquering a kingdom and getting two books was better than getting none.

8

The day started with raining. The incessant rain didn't stop even in the evening. Villagers in Athuraliya knew that there was going to be a flood when it poured this way. And they were ready for a flood.

In the evening Batto Vidane stepped into the courtyard amidst the heavy rain sheltering his head with an alocacia leaf to go to Podi Mahattaya's boutique. He took with him the rush bag and an empty bottle to bring kerosene oil. Redi Nenda knew that Batto Vidane didn't have money with him.

Batto Vidane returned home after a while. He crossed the stile and stepped into the veranda throwing away the alocacia leaf from his hand. He entered the house and gave the kerosene oil bottle and the bag to Redi Nenda. Redi Nenda placed the bag on the ground and opened it and then lifted her head and looked at Batto's face. There were several items like dry fish, sugar and flour.

"Why have you got so much? How are we going to repay this?" asked Redi Nenda lifting her head and looking at Batto's face.

Water started to flow all over the places by dusk. The river filled with water by the afternoon and started to overflow. The tar road was covered with flood waters.

The rain did not stop it was pouring continuously. Frogs too started to croak incessantly. Adding to that, the noise of the crickets provided harmony to the music of the frogs. The river was flowing hissing like a ferocious serpent.

Everytime it flooded, it was a bad experience for Athuraliya villagers. Their paddy fields and lands got washed away in the flood. Their hearts would be engulfed with fear. If the flood waters increased their abodes would be lost; therefore, the people who lived by the river used to spend sleepless nights, as they knew if the water level went up their houses would be washed away. Batto also thought that their house might be washed away by the flood at any time. Everyone in Batto's family thought, if their wattle and daub house got soaked in water, the clay in the wall would get washed and the whole house would collapse on to them. If such a thing happened everything would be finished. Everyone would die at once. They were praying to God to protect them and their house from the flood. "Dear God, may the flood level not go up," they prayed.

Rain stopped by midnight. But there was no sign of relief from flood. The following morning the sky was clear and they could see clear and bright sunrise.

A sunny day after heavy rains brought happiness to villagers and also to Batto.

Redi Nenda fell sick during the day and started to vomit. She got an allergy from something she ate. Batto Vidane did not take it seriously at the outset but he started to worry when she vomited three to four times. "Babi, why don't you prepare some ginger juice for

Amma," asked Batto Vidane and went out to get some coffee from the neighboring house. He soon came back and placed what he brought on Babi's hand asking, "If she is not good yet, give her a cup of coffee."

Redi Nenda's vomiting didn't stop even from coffee and her condition worsened with fever.

"Give some more ginger juice; I'll go bring Weda Mahattaya." Batto Vidane ordered others to treat to her with some more ginger juice and ran out of the house for the local doctor Weda Mahattaya's house.

Everyone knew that Redi Nenda's illness was serious this time. While there was a big flood coming around; a member of the family falling ill is not good. It was a fearful experience for a family like Batto's. Samy, Babi and Addin all three understood the fear that their father had felt. But they were helpless to do anything.

Weda Mahattaya was at home. He gave Batto some black coloured tablets for Redi Nenda to drink with ginger juce. Batto clutched it into his hand and ran towards home. When he stepped on to the verandah he called Babi.

"Chop a piece of ginger quickly". Addin got the lead and ran to the courtyard before Babi. He ripped off a piece of ginger from the ginger plant at the corner of the courtyard. Babi dissolved the tablet in ginger juice in a spoon and gave it to Redi Nenda to drink. All of them wished that Redi Nenda should be fine after the medicine. But it was only a whim. She vomited time and time again and her fever too didn't subside.

They had only one thing left to do. That was to take her to the Matara General Hospital. The road leading to the hospital was also flooded. It was difficult for a vehicle to go from Kadduwa to Athuraliya. Sometimes it was possible to go to Matara from Kadduwa.

It was even doubtful whether the buses were functioning due to the flood. Batto knew that there was a car on hire at the Kadduwa market. But they would charge a lot to go to Matara in that car. How could he find such a huge sum of money to hire the car? If he was somehow able to take the patient to Kadduwa, he was sure of taking her from there to Matara hospital.

"Babi, get ready to take your mother to Matara, I'll just come back." Batto ordered Babi and rushed out of the house. He passed the stile and walked fast in the flood on the narrow tar road towards Podi Mahattaya's boutique. Babi and Addin looked at him and they knew that he was going to borrow some money from Podi Mahattaya. If there was any urgency Batto used to borrow some money from Podi Mahattaya.

But this time Batto had to return home empty handed. He did not loss courage and walked into the house straightaway. He opened the table drawer and took out a rusty box. Batto knew that Redi Nenda's most important belongings were kept there. He searched thoroughly inside the box and took out a tiny pair of earrings. Redi Nenda got it a few years ago from a house in the village at the coming of age celebration of a girl. Those had been the earrings that the girl of that house was wearing when she attained age. Redi Nenda has been protecting those earrings like a cobra that protects a gem. But when Batto took it out from the drawer, she didn't utter a word.

Batto Vidane took it and stepped into the courtyard quickly. Babi and Addin who were waiting for him could understand what he was going to do. This time, he returned home with money. Redi Nenda got dressed in white clothes. Babi washed an empty bottle and placed it in her hands.

"Ok, let's leave," Batto led the way. Flood waters were flowing and making a lot of noise.

"You should not leave the house as Babi will be alone at home," ordered Batto to Addin.

Batto Vidane started walking in the flood with his wife. They could not get any vehicle from Kadduwa. They had to wait for some time there.

'I cannot bear this situation,' Batto thought. So he was anyway determined to go to Matara even by a hired car. By that time Redi Nenda had got a bit of a relief from vomiting. Anyway they could find a vehicle to go to Matara.

It was already dark when they returned home with the medicine. Babi had lighted the bottle lamp at home and prepared a pot of porridge for her mother. Redi Nenda was only given porridge for dinner. Not only her, all others that night had the same porridge for dinner.

The next morning Redi Nenda was feeling better and her fever had gone down. Even the flood waters had started to subside.

9

Mahatun who was an assistant of Bala Mahattaya of Palliyagedara came riding a bicycle, stopped in front of Batto's house and placed one leg on the stile while still sitting on the bicycle. He called Addin who was in the courtyard.

"Hey, come here." Addin walked to the stile on the command of Mahatun who was on the bicycle stationed there. "Tell your mother to keep the suit of Bala Mahattaya of Palliyegedara ready by evening."

"Amma is not well," said Addin.

"I don't know, Bala Mahattaya told me to inform you," replied Mahatun and sped away.

Addin ran in to the house and conveyed the message to his mother.

Palliyegedara was one of the honourable and rich families in the village.

"How can we prepare his suit by the evening? Ever since the dirty clothes were brought it has been raining, in addition there is flood all over. How can we wash them? They cannot understand the difficulties we face here. They don't feel for others," Redi Nenda said.

"There are some clothes of Bala Mahattaya to be washed it seems. But they said that suit will be collected in the evening" Redi Nenda said in a rough tone that could be heard by Batto who was at the rearside of the house.

"Hmmm," said Batto and hurried to the Wellawa in the kictchen and put down all the clothes. Among them he selected Bala Mahattaya's white *banyan* and the sarong. He took the two pieces to the tar road covered with flood water. Then he dipped the clothes in the flood water three to four times and brought them back. The sky was gloomy. Water was clear as the flood was subsiding. However, the clothes did not dry until the evening. Batto put fire to the hearth with two to three coconut shells. Then he collected the charcoal made from burnt coconut shells and put it inside the iron. Vidane first ironed on a dried banana leaf to check wheather it is properly heated or not. He used to do it every time before starting to iron clothes.

"Ironing clothes is not something that anyone can perform," Redi Nenda sometimes told Addin and Samy.

"You need a lot of strength to do it."

During other days they heated the iron to iron a lot of clothes. But they heated the iron that day to iron only two pieces. Since those were still wet Batto had to dry them with the iron.

"We do this sort of things, because we are born to a low caste, what to do!" said Redi Nenda in a sad tone while looking at Mahatun riding away with Bala Mahattaya's suit. But that was just an empty statement.

"It is no point talking all that, that's the nature of this world" said Vidane while moving inside the house.

If they wouldn't have prepared Bala Mahattaya's clothes that day on time, they knew about the repercussions they would have to face. Redi Nenda still remembers how they got scolded in bad, filthy language when one day they could not return Bala Mahattaya's clothes on time. He came before the Batto's house and put one leg to the stile of the fence and scolded them bitterly mentioning their low caste, Redi Nenda remembered. At that time too Vidane had not uttered a single word in reply; it was Redi Nenda who had pleaded to Bala Mahattaya, "Please sir, Vidane has got his hand injured. That's why we could not return your clothes on time. You should not scold us this way. I will somehow keep your clothes ready by tomorrow morning".

But Bala Mahattaya didn't stop scolding. He was drunk at that time. Later the villagers blamed him. Though people spoke on his behalf, Batto Vidane's fear never dispelled.

10

Batto Vidane didn't speak much, as he believed that being from a lower caste he was not a man of any importance. He very rarely spoke of anything important. Even if he spoke, it would be about something painful that had been lingering in his heart for a long time. He had loads of such things in his heart, but he could rarely put his emotions into words.

There was one such incident that loomed in his heart even till date. He sometimes related the incident to Addin and Samy. When the moonlight used to fall brightly inside the verandah, on those nights they sat on a step of the verandah and talked about different issues related to them. Everyone enjoyed the chit-chat under the moonlight. Those were the times when Batto used to speak and tell stories about incidents that had happened to them. On the the other days too they often used to chat by the light of the bottle lamp sitting on a step of the verandah. Whenever they had no work during the night, they used to take the dinner early and sit on the steps in the verandah to listen to Batto's painful stories.

That incident was one of very painful ones for both Redi Nenda and Batto. People in the village till date blamed Bala Mahattaya for it. Bala Mahattaya of Palliye

Gedara was affluent and powerful. People blamed him for showing off his powers to an innocent man like Batto. Everyone showed pity on him and said, "poor man."

When that incident occurred, Samy was five or six years old. The other two were yonger. Addin was a toddler at that time.

Batto's family, before they moved into their present place, were staying in a house that belonged to Bala Mahattaya. That house was situated upstream of the river and hence was closer to the river. It was a small thatched house. To the right of it there was a small area to cook their meals. Firewood, coconut leaves and other wood were kept in that area.

One night when they were just about to go to sleep, Babi saw a rising flame between the roof and the wall of the house. She showed that to Batto, "*Appochchi*, there?" As soon as he saw it, Batto jumped and ran out of the house shouting and asked everyone to leave the house. Batto never showed such a rush ever, all in the house ran out of the house at once.

"A stench of kerosene, Oh My God! Someone has set fire to our house!" Batto at once realised what had happened, but there was no time to explain to others about it. He jumped and took a bucket and started throwing water to put out the fire. Others were shouting and helped Batto to put water to the fire. In not time their neighbours flocked at their house hearing the noise. All helped him to extinguish the fire within a few minutes. Luckily the fire could not enter the house. Only the kitchen was burnt down from the fire.

Batto knew that Bala Mahattaya had been wanting to chase them from his land for a long time. Bala Mahattaya had a lot of land in the village. But they were all abandoned and overgrown with trees and dense forest. Bala Mahattaya was prejudiced and was under the fear that Batto would not leave his land and will acquire his land one day. Batto thought that Bala Mahattaya was trying to remove his family from this land because of that.

Batto heard that Bala Mahattaya had once told at the boutique that "Now that Batto has got two boys. When they are grown up, we will not be able to get our land back and we will not even be able to get even a single coconut grown on that land."

Batto never wanted to acquire Bala Mahattaya's land. He was ready to leave the land meekly as a rat whenever he would have been asked to. What he wanted was only a place to stay to earn a living. When Bala Mahattaya requested him to vacate the land, Batto Vidane never objected to it.

"Sir, we will be leaving this land as soon as we find another place to stay," said Batto Vidane to Bala Mahattaya. It was an innocent and humble request.

It was however difficult to find an alternative land for Batto to be relocated. Therefore, their evacuation too got delayed. However, after that incident their departure got precipitated.

From there, their next destination was on a land that belonged to Mahagedara *Ralahami*. He allowed Batto to stay on his land with a pretext that if Batto's family will be living on that land, thieves would not come to steal coconuts from the coconut trees. So Mahagedara *Ralahami* thought he would be able to protect his coconut trees from thieves. However, he showed that he gave him the land on sympathetic grounds. And he was generous to allow Batto's family to settle on that land temporary.

"I allowed you to live on my land because I feel sorry for you".

"Ok, sir," Batto bent forward to pay his regard to Mahagedara *Ralahami* accepting the decision.

There was a small thatched house on the edge of the coconut land. The former tenant of the house was a traditional drummer called Angunne. They were also a low caste family. The house got vacated as he went to live in his daughter's house. The house, therefore, had been abandoned for months. On some rainy days, people used to tie their cows in the verandah of the house. Other than the verandah that house had only a single room. There were owl droppings all over the house as it was abandoned for some time. The roof of the house was also decaying and there were cracks on the walls.

Before they moved into the new place, they built a small kitchen and repaired the walls and the roof of the house. Redi Nenda went to consult Nakath Mama, the village astrololger, to get the auspicious time to start living in the new house. She took with her some betel leaves for him and asked to prepare an auspicious time. They started to live in the new house by the dawn of the day according to the auspicious time designated by Nakath Mama.

11

The news of the appointment of a new principal for the school and the retirement of the old one spread like wildfire in the village. There was a buzz among the villagers that the new principal was young and competent.

"The Village school is getting a new principal." When some of the villagers were discussing the arrival of the new principal, Batto was at the village boutique. He was squatting in the corner of the verandah of the boutique. He never sat on the bench. The bench was for other villagers to sit on. That was the custom among villagers.

Addin and Samy wore shirts for the first time in their life after the arrival of the new principal of the school. It all happened during the first morning assembly of the new principal. By that time they had already passed the age of wearing shirts to the school. Therefore, they still used to wear a sarong to school and did not wear anything to cover their upper body. There were only seven or eight such boys in the school. All of them belonged to low castes, either washer families or drummer families. All others wore shirts to cover their upper body. On the first day the new principal arrived at the school, he called for a special morning assembly for all the students in the school ground. Among the students, the principal saw some boys like Addin in the assembly with their upper body bare. Except them, all others were in shirts. He was surprised.

"Why are you without shirts?" asked the principal pointing his finger towards them. No one replied and as they were embarassed. Later, one of the teachers who was standing close to the principal murmered something into his ear. He understood everything. The principal then ordered them to come to school in shirts from the very next day. After that Addin and Samy got the right to wear clothes to cover their upper body. Though Addin didn't have any proper dress to wear, he was nevertheless happy about the equal rights granted for all students. Even Batto and his wife were happy with the decision given by the new principal.

The new principal brought new light to the school. He was young and spent most of his time in the school. He was instrumental in forming a number of societies in the school such as the literary union and the Buddhist society. Students were encouraged in their studies.

Samy, the eldest child of Batto's family didn't show much interest in studies. Even Addin did not show interest in his studies in his early ages, but slowly changed his attitude after the arrival of the new principal. He started to develop an interest for his studies and performed well in all the lessons. However, he did not have sufficient books and Batto did not have enough money to buy school materials for him. But Addin still managed his schooling and studied hard.

Earlier both Addin and Samy considered the school as a place that did not belong to them. But now there impression began changing gradually. Earlier they used to remain aloof from all the activities in their class and the school. But now they were confident of moving forward.

That day, after the Rural Development soceity's meeting a few people stepped into Podi Mahattaya's boutique. Two or three people were sitting on a bench and Batto was squatting on the ground at the edge of the verendah.

"It is good for the village that the new principal is the Chairman of the Rural development society," said Piyadasa who was sitting on the bench.

"We have forgotten about the need of a bus service to the village until the principal suggested," said Diyonis taking the newspaper to his hand.

"How good it would be to have a bus in this village;" when Piyadasa said loudly another one agreed to that, "that's right!"

Batto was listening without uttering a single word while all others were talking about the rural development society and the new proposals. He was backward in suggesting any idea among others.

Though there was lively discussion about the new bus, there was no sign of a new bus coming to the village.

12

Samy stopped schooling after he spent two years in grade five. He went to school not because studying was his main motive but because he thought that all others were doing the same. Both Batto and Redi Nenda knew about it well too. Therefore, no one at home was interested in sending him to school. Samy, who stopped schooling, spent most of his time outside his house. On some days he used to leave home early in the morning and return home when it was dark. He was initially in the habit of earning some money by plucking coconuts and jack fruits, and later on he started idling at Podi Mahattaya's boutique. Later, he got a chance to axe firewood in Podi Mahattaya's brick factory. Podi Mahattaya was able to use Samy for his other business activities after he joined the brick factory.

Podi Mahattaya was a rich, powerful figure in the village. His boutique was managed by an assistant. His illicit liquor business was managed by another assistant. He had enough of assistants for his work.

Samy's journey which started with axing firewood ended up engaging himself in Podi Mahattaya's *Kasippu* business. His *Kasippu* distillary business was carried out very secretly, hiding all signs of it from the police. Samy to him was not just an assistant but was also a faithful assistant in all sorts of his secret affairs.

Samy crossed the stile and passed the courtyard. Redi Nenda was leaning on to the door frame and was watching him coming towards the house. His dirty sarong was folded up in to two and his upper body was naked.

"Whole day you are out, where do you go every day?" Redi Nenda asked Samy who was entering the house. It was getting dark. Batto was sitting squatting in the edge of the verandah. A pile of clothes washed and dried were stacked on the bed in the other corner of the verandah ready to be ironed.

Samy did not say anything. "You leave home every day like a man goes for a job and come in the night. Can't you help your father at least in ironing clothes," continued Redi Nenda.

"I have some other work to do," replied Samy going into the house.

"Yes, you have, to lay idle and roam here and there," replied Redi Nenda

"Do you also want me to slap clothes on the stone? It is better to earn a living by theft rather than washing clothes. Can you even find money to take three meals a day by slapping clothes on the stone? I can't do that job," said Samy stretching himself on the bed in the verandah. The smell of sweat emanating from his body was felt by Redi Nenda and Batto.

"Stop that talking," said Batto to Redi Nenda who was listening to their conversation patiently. His tone implied that he had no controlling power over him though he was his own son. He had a feeling that he had no right to say anything about him. On the other hand Batto was not in a position to do anything against Samy, because Samy did not listen to anyone at home.

Unlike Addin, Samy never wanted to help his mother in her work. He never carried dirty clothes to the river for his mother nor did he ever carry washed clothes to the house from the river. He never helped to dry clothes nor ironed them. Batto had doubts since long, whether Samy would ever continue this job they had been doing for generations. But even for Samy there was no alternative available to make a living. Batto believed that Addin and Samy too should continue the same job after his death. If Samy refused to accept washing clothes there would not be anybody in the village to do it, and both Batto and Redi Nenda thought that the job has been entrusted upon them by some unforeseen rule. They believed that everyone in their family had to follow that rule without any deviation.

However, amidst all those beliefs Batto believed that he had no ability to control Samy's behavior. Thus he allowed him to do anything and go anywhere he wanted to and kept quiet.

Batto liked to see Samy working for Podi Mahattaya as he was a well-off man in the village. Working for such a person would bring some status to him. On certain days Samy rode Podi Mahattaya's cart and on some days, he measureed grocery in his boutique. On certain occasions, Samy worked on Podi Mahattaya's paddy fields. Looking at all these, Batto said, "Samy is doing well now."

With time, Samy was able to win Podi Mahattaya's heart and became his best subordinate. He turned out to be the best assistant in his *Kasippu* business. By that time he had become a stalwart youth. Podi Mahattaya had been able to identify all his capabilities towards his underground business.

"You need not go home even at night; you can sleep in the boutique. I will tell your *Appochchi*," Podi Mahattaya offered Samy.

"No need to tell *Appochchi*, I will stay," replied Samy.

For Samy, his father was an unimportant figure.

From that day onwards, Samy went home seldomly, may be once a month or so. He had no need to go to home. He liked working for Podi Mahattaya than washing clothes or being at home.

He became the custodian of Podi Mahattaya's *Kasippu* business. He did the business better than Podi Mahattaya expected. He boiled the mixture of liquor in a cauldron. Then he used the vapor emanating from it using a pipeline laid under river water connected to the cauldron. The vapor turned into a liquid and then it was bottled. The bottles were hidden in the river water. Everyone called this liquor as *Kasippu*. They sold *Kasippu* to the buyers who came to their place to drink. When he used to return from work in the evening he got a rich plate of rice from Podi Mahattaya's place just as his other assistants. He slept on a camp bed in the verandah of the boutique.

13

When Addin reached grade eight he had become one of the best students in the class. He even looked matured than his age. He was leading in all the subjects in the class. He reached that level without sufficient books and clothing.

One day, Addin was alone in the class. He was doing some work sitting alone on a bench. All others in the class had left the room. He was startled by a voice; a girl was standing in front of him. He lifted his head and looked at her. It was Sumana and her presence made him look around.

"Here, take these two exercise books. I saw that your math book is finished and you were writing on the back cover. I have a lot of books," said Sumana, extending two exercise books towards him. Addin's hand went towards the books automatically. But at the same he was frightened. So he replied instantly, "No, I don't want, I have exercise books."

"No, that's Ok, no one would see," she pleaded again looking around.

Addin took the two books and quickly hid them under his books. Though he was excited about the gift, still he got up from his chair and started to look around.

Sumana was not a bright student and was a playful girl in the class. Her father ran a grocery in the Kadduwa market. The villagers called her father as Madduma Mahattaya. Sumana was not interested in studies but was more into fancy things.

This is not the first instance when Addin realied that she gave him special attention. During one instance, when a name of a boy was to be proposed for some work in the class, Sumana proposed Addin's name.

Addin knew that he was Batto's son who belonged to the washers' caste. Therefore, he mingled with children of other families in the village with caution. He always opted to be aloof in the class. He inherited this habit of selecting the place he deserves from his parents. He saw how his father behaved when he was at Podi Mahattaya's boutique or any other place in the village.

Podi Mahattaya's boutique was the largest in the area. There were grocery items on one side and tea was served on the other. Racks were filled with grocery items. There were two or three chairs and a bench in the verendah. People gathered there not only to buy grocery but also to stop for a friendly chat or to be aware of the news around. It was the meeting place of the village. When Batto felt bored at home he used to go to Podi Mahattaya's boutique. Though, there were ample empty chairs or a vacant bench, he never sat on them. He always used to squat in a corner of the verandah closer to the garden. He opened his mouth only when someone asked him something. Otherwise, he would listen to what others had say. He would squat and listen to what others talked, like a buffalo lying in mud.

Addin seeing his father's behavior would never go forward for anything in the school. He always kept himself at a distance from other children. Therefore, he had to be meek in front of Sumana too.

Though, Addin was submissive, others in the class had a sense of Sumana's intention. Therefore, children had started teasing Sumana calling after Addin's name. Addin knew that but even that did not make any change in Addin's behavior, because Addin knew that those things are prohibited for them who belonged to the washers' caste. He wanted to mind his own business and so kept quiet.

On one evening, only Addin and Babi were at home. Redi Nenda had gone to distribute washed clothes and collect dirty clothes. Both Batto Vidane and Samy were also not at home.

All of a sudden, someone on a bicycle stopped in front of their house and started shouting. Addin was near the window. Peering out of the window, he recognised that it was Madduma Mahattaya. He was his classmate, Sumana's father. An incident that happened in the school on that day came to his mind at once. He was nervous.

"Filthy Radav, if you want to take a woman, find another matching Rada woman for you. Son of a bitch, where is that bloody rascal. Where have you gone! Where is your father? I'll teach you a good lesson. Do we give our girls in marriage to Radav?" Addin heard the angry voice of Madduma Mahattaya and he realised that there was every reason for him to be angry. He stayed curled and silent in the same place like a rat. But

Babi went near the door and peeped her head towards the road.

'Now, the news will spread like wildfire in the village', Addin thought. 'Now I would not be able to step out from this house. And I would be beaten up when my parents return home and no one would believe that I was innocent. It was a very serious situation; he became restless and could not think of what to do.

Two new exercise books given by Sumana were still lying there with his other books.

"Don't think that this is the end of the incident. I will never give this up easily. Because of you Radavas, our girls could not go to school. These rascals are coming behind them. I won't allow you to stay in this village," Madduma Mahattaya kept shouting. Babi and Addin were frightened and curled up in a corner of the house until he left.

After Madduma Mahattaya left, Addin quietly took the two exercise books Sumana had given to him, ran out of the house and hid them under a bush in the grove at the corner of the coconut land behind the house. He came out of the grove and did not return home.

He knew that Batto would punish him severely if he went home. Though Batto was a silent man, he got angry like a devil. On the other hand, now Addin would not be able to go to school from the next day, because of this incident. As everyone in the village would know the whole story by then so he decided to go somewhere without going home. He crossed the grove adjoining the paddy field and started walking on the gravel road on the other side. He had no idea where he should be heading to, but he was walking forward without turning back.

Batto and Redi Nenda got to know about the incident from Babi only after they returned home in the evening. They thought that Addin might return home after dark in the evening. But he did not return home even after dark. Redi Nenda thought that he would be hiding somewhere in the coconut grove, scared of his father. Then she went to the rear side of the house in the dark and called out loudly.

"Addin...! Addin...! Come home!"

Though she called his name continuously for long he did not return home. Batto and Redi Nenda thought that he should be hiding somewhere closer to the house. But he did not return home until dawn. The next morning Redi Nenda thought that he might have run away from home and told Batto that he should go search for Addin. But where would they find him? No one knew in which direction he had headed. They were at a loss as to what should be done.

"Where should I search for him? If you want I can search in our sister's place and check if he went there or not."

"Ok, let's go and search then."

The next morning Batto Vidane left for his sister's house which was located about four miles away. He walked the distance at a stretch. But he returned home without any information of Addin.

Addin had not gone there. Even from the neighbours they could not get any clue on Addin's disappearance.

Other than that someone had seen him going towards Kadduwa, they heard no further news of him.

"I feel sorry for the boy," said Batto shedding a heavy breath while squatting on the edge of the veranda when he returned home after being exhausted by his search of Addin the whole day. Not only Redi Nenda but also the others at home heard the voice of Batto Vidane. It was evening and it was getting dark. At the same time they heard the shoutings of someone afar. Everyone directed their ears towards the noise to understand what it was.

"Babi, you go inside the house," Redi Nenda commanded her daughter. She felt that something unpleasant was going to happen again. She was frightened.

"I will kill those, rascals," it was a familier voice.

"Amma, it is our brother, isn't it?" Babi identified her brother Samy's voice.

"This is a strange law here, though we are Radavas, don't we have a right to live in this village? If any of them try to hurt anyone of us, I will kill them all;" all three in the house knew that Samy was hinting at Madduma Mahattaya. Samy crossed over the stile with difficulty and he was stammering; everyone knew that he was drunk.

"What has happened to you Samy?" Redi Nenda stepped into the courtyard to help him and noticed that he had a dagger in his hand.

"You have nothing to do with this, you should go and sleep," she placed her hand on his shoulder and escorted him into the house. Babi also moved closer to her mother.

14

"From next month I must go to work in Hamu Mahattaya's Estate," said Batto squatting at the corner of the verandah facing the courtyard in a tone that Redi Nenda could hear. "...so that I will be able to get some money," he added. Redi Nenda understood what Batto said. She was selecting ironed clothes to distribute for the following day. She looked at Batto and saw him squatting in the verandah. That was his usual way of sitting there. Their courtyard was filled with moonlight. Coconut trees around the house were moving with the wind. Shadows made by the moonlight were also moving with the moving trees. Beyond the courtyard moonlight was flowing all over the coconut land. The following day is the full moon day, Redi Nenda thought.

"Can you do manual labour in the estate...?" asked Redi Nenda out of concern. She knew well that hardships were aggravating at home. They knew that they would not be able to earn a proper living by their job. The small income they earned was also not enough even for their food. They asked for a jack fruit or bread fruit from a house in the village when they visited to collect or distribute clothes to fill up the gap of the cost of their food.

"Who would wash these clothes then? How can I do it all by myself?" asked Redi Nenda.

"Washing clothes is not a big issue. If someone washes them during the day time, I can come in the evening and iron the clothes. That is not the problem. Real problem is how I will do heavy work without any practice," said Batto.

"I don't know, we somehow need to do something about this, if not we have to face more and more difficulties," said Redi Nenda.

"Now I feel the absence of Addin. If he were here we could have handed over a part of our work to him. Loss of him, I feel like losing a half of the house," Batto Vidane said sorrowfully.

Batto left home early morning for work at Hamu Mahattaya's estate and returned home at dusk. Hamu Mahattaya's estate was located two miles away from Batto's house. By the time he returned home he was tired. Redi Nenda therefore did not feel like getting the clothes ironed by him. When the ironing got delayed they got a scolding from customers.

"What's the meaning of this, it has been a long time, but we still haven't got our clothes back," everyone scolded Redi Nenda for not returning the clothes on the due date.

"Very sorry, Hamine, my husband goes for manual labour. He doesn't have time to iron clothes," Redi Nenda pleaded before them.

"That's a funny justification. We give you money for washing our clothes, don't we? You can gain nothing by going after more money," blamed the customers. They know that they are giving only a few rupees to Redi Nenda for a year and they hid the fact in their minds.

"Oh! No Hamine, he goes for work due to hardships at home". Redi Nenda knew about how much they get paid for washing clothes. But, she had no strength to retort at those who scolded her. Instead, she pleaded in front of them by promising to return the clothes as soon as possible.

It was at that time that there was the death of Maha *Ralahami* at Mahagedara. Maha *Ralahami* of Mahagedara was the former village headman and had been a noble man in the village and the news of his death spread in the village by giving the people in the village an opportunity to demonstrate their allegiance to the family. He was living like a lion in that village. He did his duty as a king of a kingdom. His son was the village headman after him and he was known as Punchi *Ralahami* among the villagers. Punchi *Ralahami* too was a noble man in the village. Everyone had high regards for him.

Batto received the message from Mahagedara to attend the funeral. He got the news from his wife. He ran to Mahagedara soon after he returned home from work in the evening.

"You should lay *Pawada* for the funeral," said Punchi *Ralahami* to Batto.

"Ok," replied Batto in a meek tone while bending forward to pay his respect to *Ralahami*. His shawl was in his hand and he kept his two hands folded behind as a form of respect.

"We anyway might need two or three people to lay *Pawada*," elaborated Punchi *Ralahami*.

Batto knew that laying *Pawada* for a funeral procession was a difficult task. They need at least two or three youth for the task. It's a long distance from *Ralahami*'s house to the cemetery and they need to lay *Pawada* covering that distance.

Batto didn't go for work the next day. Instead he went to see his sister in the adjoining village to get help from her two sons and another person for the task of laying *Pawada* for the funeral. They too were well experienced in the task.

Laying of *Pawada* at the funeral was successfully done as they expected. Two sons of Batto's sister were very helpful for the process. They laid *Pawada* for the funeral procession which was headed by the monks and the team of drummers. The coffin bearers were walking slowly on *Pawada* behind the monks. Once the group of coffin bearers walked on the *Pawada*, their duty was to collect the cloth and pass it on to one of their members who was walking in front of the funeral procession. From there onwards, they would again hold it from the two sides and spread it on the track again for the coffin bearers to walk on. They would do the same thing repetitively until they reached the cemetery. It was such a tiring exercise for them.

On the next day of *Ralahami*'s funeral, Batto received fifty rupees from Punchi *Ralahami* as his payment for laying *Pawada* at the funeral. He had to give ten rupees each to the boys who assisted him to lay Pawada.

"It is not good if I don't give something to them," Batto told Redi Nenda.

Batto also received another thing from *Ralahami*'s home. It was the bed that Maha *Ralahami* had been using before his death.

"You may take this," said Punchi *Ralahami* pointing to the bed that was kept in the corner of the kitchen. It was one of the old customs of a funeral house in the village. Therefore, it was not at all a surprise to Batto. But he had no guts to ask for it. It was customary to give the bed of the dead person to the washerman in the village. Even this custom was practiced only among the well-to-do people in the village.

The bed was carried to the river by two people, and washed well. Then he kept it in the courtyard to dry up and brought it inside the house after three days. It was an old bed but looked rich. Therefore, he kept it in the other corner of the verandah. Now there were two beds in the verandah.

Batto could not go to work in the estate for three days due to the funeral of Maha Gedara Maha *Ralahami*. He got a harsh scolding from the Estate Manager on the fourth day when he went for work.

"If you really want to work, you may come; otherwise, you can stay at home. You cannot work irregularly like this. I will dismiss you from work after informing Hamu Mahattaya," Estate Manager warned him.

"Sir, I had to go to lay Pawada for *Ralahami*'s funeral, that is our ancestral duty," pleaded Batto bending.

But he received no mercy from the manager.

"I won't excuse you. If you do one thing, do it properly. You cannot do two things at once."

Batto knew that he had to work at the estate to earn money and overcome his hardships. He realised that it was difficult to do both the jobs simultaneously.

"I cannot take scolding from villagers like this everyday. We should wash and return clothes on time. You will have to iron the clothes," said worried Redi Nenda

"Hmm, Ok!" Batto said releasing a sigh and squatting at a corner of the verandah.

The next day he went to Hamu Mahattaya's place to bring the week's salary. Thereafter, he never went to work there.

15

That evening, Batto Vidane stepped into the verandah impatiently like never before. He peeped from the open door and couldn't find Redi Nenda in the house. Then he went to the back door and peeped into the kitchen. Though the sun had already gone down he could see some kind of light inside the house.

Redi Nenda was squatting near the hearth. There was something boiling in the pot on the hearth. The glow from the fire has giving more reddish colour to her face. Batto's face was also lighted with the fire from the hearth when he peeped in to the kitchen. He stayed at the door, placing his two hands on the door frame.

"Hey, look here?" Batto broke Redi Nenda's attention. She understood that something had happened. She turned her head and saw his impatient face through the light emitted by the fire. Though it was dark inside the house, there was still light outside the house.

"What happened?" asked Redi Nenda a little puzzled.

"Addin is working in a hotel in Matara".

"Really? Who told you?" now Redi Nenda was startled too.

"Yes, he's making tea in a boutique it seems; Martin Mahattaya told me near the boutique. He has seen him there."

"Since he left home, he could not even send us a letter".

"It has been almost six-seven months since he left us. If you know the place he stays, why don't you go and bring him here," Redi Nenda pleaded to Batto.

"Let's see in two-three days," replied Batto.

"No point in seeing, go and fetch him here," Redi Nenda pleaded again.

"Who knows may be he would also not come home just like Samy," said Batto in a sad and lethargic tone.

"No, he cannot stay anywhere for long. He always wanted to live with us. Even now he must be finding it difficult, I guess," Redi Nenda said in one go.

This news of Addin got a new lease of life to Batto, Redi Nenda and Babi. And also whenever they spoke on this, their courage renewed.

"Need to find some money to go to Matara," said Batto to Redi Nenda. However, his journey got delayed for few days due to financial difficulties.

That day Batto and Redi Nenda were slapping clothes on the stone and washing at the river bank from morning to noon. Turn by turn they slapped clothes on the stone like playing to a tune, looking at the stone without talking. Clear river water flowed down slowly.

"Amme!" They were startled by a loud shout from Babi who came running through the coconut land and reached them at the river.

Both Redi Nenda and Batto stopped slapping clothes, raised their heads and looked at Babi.

"Why are you shouting?" asked Redi Nenda seeing Babi's face which looked excited and happy.

"Malli has come," said Babi in an excited tone.

"Addin!" Redi Nenda's face lit up with a smile. "Why didn't he come here?" Redi Nenda asked with the cloth still in her hand.

"He said, he can't," said Babi

"Maybe he is shy," said Batto starting to slap the cloth again on the stone.

Redi Nenda dropped the cloth in her hand in the river water, rinsed and threw it on the heap of the washed clothes at the bank. Then she washed her hands from the river water quickly.

"You may slap the rest, I'll go and see him," Redi Nenda said to Batto while washing her hands. Then she wiped her hands on the clothes she was wearing and left quickly with Babi.

Redi Nenda could not control her joy seeing Addin who was sitting on the bed in the verandah. Her overflowing joy ended up in tears.

Addin was sitting on the bed which was received from Maha Gedara after his funeral. He was looking at the floor with a bent head. He did not raise his head.

"Oh! Addin, did you not miss us all these days," said Redi Nenda crying and drawing his head closer to her bosom. Tears were pouring down from her eyes.

Seeing it, Babi too started crying. She turned her head away to hide tears in her eyes.

Addin didn't step outside the house for few days, shyness and fear were still haunting his mind.

Batto also never faced Addin, but inquired more and more about him either from Redi Nenda or Babi.

Though, he worked in a hotel for six to seven months, yet he could not earn anything from it. The hotel owner gave him only food in return of his labour. He was not given a cent as salary. Realising the fruitlessness of his stay there, he ran away from the hotel and came back home.

16

The rainy season that year commenced a little early. The rain that started in the evening continued for a few hours. Sometimes, it rained the whole night. At times when it rained continuously for more than a week or so, villagers knew that it was a sign of a flood. Every thing around them including vegetation and the villages were soaked in rain water.

"Looks like it's going to be a flood this time,"said Batto, to Redi Nenda while stepping out on the verandah from inside the house.

It was customary for them to wash all the dirty clothes soon and distribute them among the owners even in rainy seasons. They knew that if rain started it would continue for several days and that it will disturb their washing process at the river.

"Ironing is barely finished. Need to go distribute them tomorrow if raining stops for a while," said Redi Nenda in the evening.

"If it gets flooded, we might not have anything to eat at home," said Redi Nenda again.

The rain became severe. The rain which poured intermittently was now pouring continuously. When it rained hard, water started to drip from the roof to the mud floor. The clay on the mud floor got washed off from the rain water.

"The thatched roof has decayed. If it will keep raining like this, it would be difficult even to live in this house," Batto alerted Redi Nenda a few days before the heavy raining started.

"If we can pass this rainy season we can survive with this roof for another five or six months," said Batto.

The rain receded by the morning. Batto who spent the whole day at home took the big handkerchief which was on the head of his bed and put it on his shoulder. Then he stepped out to go to Podi Mahattaya's boutique. Rain drops hanging at the end of the leaves of the trees fell on the ground with a *sata-sata* sound.

The rain started again after he left home. There were signs of another harsh rain. The sky was filled with dark clouds. Frogs on the river bank were croaking incessantly.

Batto borrowed a gunny sack from Podi Mahattaya's boutique and sheltered his head from it and started walking back home while the rain receded a bit. He stepped on to the verandah in the rain placing the gunny sack he put on his head on the short wall at the end of the verandah. The gunny sack and his sarong were all soaked in water.

He sat on the bed at the verandah. Redi Nenda was inside the house.

"Look here, there's water up to the hip, at the Bogaha junction." Batto spoke in a disappointed and helpless tone. With this noise Redi Nenda came out to the verandah and made a look afar beyond the stile of the courtyard. Still it was raining. There seemed no end. Crickets and frogs started making noises continuously. That was a clear sign of a severe flood. Both Batto and Redi Nenda had that understanding.

"Looks like it's going to be a severe flood this time," said Redi Nenda.

"It's better to get ready. Podi Mahattaya's courtyard got flooded in no time," Batto peeped into the house and asked Babi to bring an areca nut seed."

While Babi was bringing it, he took out a small knife which was tucked in his waist. It used to be one of his habits to carry a knife just as a woman is used to wear earrings. He put a betel leaf with a piece of areca nut and a bit of lime into his mouth.

At the same time Addin entered in to the courtyard from the rear side of the house. He was covering his head with a big alocacia leaf. Water flowed from the alocasia leaf and poured from his elbow to the floor.

"Why are you getting wet?" Redi Nenda saw him and asked.

"There, flooded over the mango tree. In a shortwhile it catches our house too," said Addin pointing his finger towards the rear side of his house. He stepped on to the verandah and stomped his foot on the floor to remove mud stuck on his leg. Then he threw away the alocacia leaf into the courtyard.

"No, the water level might not come up to our house," said Batto in a doubtful tone. But Redi Nenda turned her head towards the river attentively. Batto felt frightened. He got up and came to the corner of the verandah and looked afar over the river. The sound of the flowing river surpassed the sound of the rain.

Flood water had been flowing through the village inundating all the low lands in the village. The river were also flowing very fast like a huge snake without any mercy. Water levels had reached near the house. Beyond that it was almost like a sea.

"It's going to be a major disaster," said Batto spitting the red saliva of the betel in the mouth to the courtyard and came back to the bed to sit there. Redi Nenda walked towards the kitchen without uttering a word.

The rain subsided a little by noon. Addin stepped into the courtyard to go see the flood. The road running in front of their house, and the area upto the river looked like an ocean. Water on the road was up to the knee level. Addin walked in the flood waters down to the road. The flood water looked muddy and full of debris. Flood was not something new to Addin and he enjoyed walking in the flood waters.The water in the river brought so many debris like garbage, tree branches, logs and what not, and it was flowing very fast washing everything on the two banks. Some of the villagers were loitering here and there to see the flood. They enjoyed flood in some way.

The rain stopped but the flood did not stop. The water level rose gradually. *Ho-ho* sound from flowing river water and the voices of the shouting and hooting by the people who had gathered to see the flood could be heard from everywhere around. Every one knew that the hooting sounds came from everywhere because of the water level of the flood going up. Those sounds were common for villagers of Athuraliya, whenever there were floods. Batto also knew that.

The flood waters reached the doorstep of Batto's house by the evening. Batto realised that the water would invade his house in a mere two or three hours' time. He knew that there was little time to be wasted. He stepped in to the courtyard and left towards Podi Mahattaya's house quickly in the flood water, with an idea in his mind.

Podi Mahattaya was at home.

"Ok, you stay there a few days. It is no matter for me." He got permission to stay with his family in the small hut which was abandoned in a land owned by Podi Mahattaya. Every time flood came to their house it was to become their temporary shelter until the flood subsided. It used to be a hut where Podi Mahattaya had his poultry farm sometime back. But now it was empty. It had a tin roof and clay walls and no doors, but there was an entrance. On certain days Podi Mahattaya's sick cow was tied in this hut. That's why there was a pile of straw in the corner of the hut. The hut usually didn't get affected by flood as it was located on an elevated land.

Batto returned home quickly.

"Ok, let's go to Podi Mahattaya's hut now itself, otherwise if someone else goes there we might lose that opportunity too," Batto told everyone.

"Put the food stuff into a bag, until I take these," commanded Redi Nenda to Babi while opening a box and empting its content into a pillow case.

"Addin, you put all those things on the floor, on the table and tie the grinding stone to the table," instructed Batto.

They placed all their unimportant belongings on the table and tied the table to the grinding stone. Batto tied the two beds together and tied those to a pillar in the verandah. All these were done to avoid them from moving away when the flood came.

There was no sign of an end to the flood. Batto kept the front and the back doors of the house open, and placed the gunny sack on his shoulder. There were some utensils and grocery inside the sack. The other things were tied in a cloth and Redi Nenda placed the pile on her head. Babi and Addin too tied the remaining stuff into clothes and prepared two piles for them to carry.

"We will have to place two or three timber pillars to support the walls if the water level goes up further," said Batto while stepping into the courtyard under flood water.

"We will come back and do it later. First we take these things there," Batto replied to his own question. Batto took the lead and Redi Nenda, Babi and Addin followed him.

They placed all their piles in a corner of the hut. Batto brought three big stones and prepared a stove. Redi Nenda swept the hut and Babi spread the mat they brought on the floor and placed some of the things they brought with them on it.

Batto sat in a corner of the mat and placed his two hands around two knees. He was not tired, but his head was filled with an excitement. Addin went down the road to see the flood.

"Do we have anything to eat for lunch?" Batto asked Redi Nenda who came closer to the stove.

"There's little rice. But I didn't take it for we might need it to prepare some porridge in case of an emergency," replied Redi Nenda.

"May you wait a second, I will prepare some plain tea," said Redi Nenda again placing a pot on the stove.

She poured a cup full of plain tea and put a little sugar on Batto's palm from the sugar bottle.

"Can't you borrow some food stuff even from Podi Mahattaya's boutique? We have to be here till the flood subsides," said Redi Nenda while putting sugar on to his palm.

"But, how can I go on for requesting more? How are we going to repay?" objected Batto to Redi Nenda's suggestion.

Redi Nenda didn't say anything further. Batto continued in his thought. He thought that it's not good to ask for some rice from anyone at this juncture for he knew that nobody volunteers to lend some rice at a time of disaster like flood. Everyone may face a difficult situation. He was sitting there for a while and got up from the mat releasing a long sigh.

He found an empty gunny bag among the things they brought from home, placed it on his shoulder and left the hut without making any comment. He walked along the gravel road located between two fences, with his head turned towards the ground. He stopped near one barbed-wire fence and looked around carefully. No one was in his sight. Not a single house was around there. He looked around again and assured that there wasn't any danger. He pulled down the barbed-wire of the fence, bent down and entered the *chena* and walked further inside. He stopped at one place for a second to look around again. There were flourishing *manioc* plants and he bent forward and pulled out a plant slowly. The plant came out with the wet soil with tuber. Within two-three seconds the whole exercise was over. Then he took the gunny sack with manioc tuber on to his shoulder. He stepped onto the gravel road quickly and returned to Podi Mahattaya's hut in one breath without looking around. He placed the sack near the stove where Redi Nenda was sitting.

Redi Nenda was at the foot of the hearth and she opened the sack. Then she peeped in and raised her head to look at Batto's face with fear like a female deer. Batto looked at Redi Nenda's face with an easy mood.

By noon, another family which was affected by the flood came to stay in Podi Mahattaya's hut. They were also refugees like Batto's family. They were a family who lived in a low land near by. They were not from a washerman's family and they belonged to a higher caste. They placed their belongings in the other corner of the hut and settled. Later they made a hearth with three boulders and started preparing their lunch.

Babi had gone to fetch a pot of water from the well next door. Redi Nenda had gone to the area which was already flooded to wash two pots. Both Addin and Batto were away to see their house under flood and therefore there was no one in the hut.

Once everyone of Batto's family was out, only the members of the second family who arrived later in the hut were there. The lady of Owita Gedara was lighting the hearth at that time. Her sixteen-year-old boy was also with her. He at once went towards the other corner of the hut. All Batto's belongings were kept in that corner. He looked around carefully. He quickly opened the gunny sack that Batto had placed in a corner and peeped into it. He took out a fresh bunch of manioc from it which was still covered with mud and closed its mouth. He, in a flash of a second came near his mother who was in the other corner of the hut and dropped the maniocs at his mother's feet and turned to go out. She looked at her son. She got up quickly and covered the maniocs from the mat.

Batto returned to the hut in the afternoon. Addin too was in the hut by that time. Redi Nenda had prepared a pot full of maniocs and scraped coconut for lunch. She served a plate to Batto. Redi Nenda knew that Batto liked to eat maniocs with scraped coconut. She served some more maniocs to his clay pot and put scraped coconut to a corner of the pot. Batto looked at the pot of hot manioc.

"From where did you get such a lot of maniocs?" asked Redi Nenda when Batto was preparing himself to sit on the mat to take his lunch.

"What's the issue with from whence I got it," Batto avoided Redi Nenda's question.

Redi Nenda knew that the maniocs are unearthed quickly before the lands get inundated because if they get affected in the flood waters the tubers turn bad and cannot be sold in the market. She thought that this too could have been such maniocs that were uprooted before the flood.

Redi Nenda saw the other family in the hut preparing for lunch. "Hamine, we have prepared maniocs for lunch, will you have some of it," Redi Nenda tried to offer them some maniocs.

"No, we too have some maniocs to boil for dinner," the lady refused Redi Nenda's offer. Redi Nenda did not know that those maniocs were also the stuff stolen from the same lot brought by Batto.

Her reply reminded Redi Nenda of the way how they are being treated by the villagers when it comes to food. Nobody in the village partakes any food or water from Batto's house. That is due their low caste, they are the people who wash and clean dirty clothes of villagers. The other family in the hut belonged to a higher caste. Redi Nenda knew that. Whenever they go to any house in the village, it was no secret the substandard way of treating by the people who are in higher castes.

"Amme," Redi Nenda turned her head towards the sound of it. The day was coming to a close. Redi Nenda was squatting at the hearth and there was a clay pot on it with water to boil. She put firewood in to the hearth.

"Oh, Samy, who showed you the road here?" He was looking at his mother with four large bread fruits hanging in his hand with coconut leaves. He kept them aside and squatted next to his mother who was at the hearth. Mother saw the knife accidentally which was tucked in his waist. It was a knife that had been banned to use.

"You would end up in the Police if they see this," seeing the knife Redi Nenda said.

"I knew that our house got flooded. That's why I came to see. Water is upto the knee level inside the house. It'll fall down. However, I have cut two Areca nut trees and fixed them to support the house." He spoke looking at his knife tucked in his waist. He had gone to see their house under flood.

"This was a flood made for ourselves," looking at the flames evolved from the hearth Redi Nenda said. Her face was red with the light of the flames.

"Where's *Appochchi*?"

"He might have gone somewhere."

"Where's *Malli*?"

"He's gone to see the flood," said Babi who was near by.

"Looks like that water won't recede till seven or eight days," said Samy while opening the pot near the hearth and inserting a piece of manioc inside his mouth.

"Have some more maniocs, there's some in the pot," Redi Nenda said to Samy.

"No, I don't want."

Samy left the hut in the evening.

17

As the rain stopped, the water level started to recede. Batto and his family could not stay more than two to three days in Podi Mahattaya's hut.

About one foot of the height of the walls of his house had been washed off by the flood and only the wooden structure was seen remaining. Even the house was still wet and there was mud all over. The floor was slippery with wet mud and they walked in the house very carefully. There was no place for them to sleep in the night as there was wet mud all over. Therefore, all four of them were sleeping on the two beds at the verandah curled up taking turns.

As the floor of the house started to dry up, Addin started to build up the walls again by applying clay on the walls. However, it took about two weeks for their lives to come back to normal.

That evening, Batto returned home from Podi Mahataya`s boutique and he brought good news for the others at home.

"Here, there is news that they are going to distribute flood aid?" he told his wife.

"To whom; now the flood has gone down," said Redi Nenda.

"For us, not anyone else. We were the people displaced from flood and suffered," Batto said.

"How do you know?"

"Notices have been published that it's given to all."

The next day he left home with Addin and returned home with a big gunny sack.

They received twelve pounds of wheat flour, two pounds of sugar and one pound of *dhal* as flood aid. It was sufficient for Batto's family to sustain for a number of days.That was a very big relief for them.

One day of the following week Redi Nenda heard another news when she was going round the houses. She brought the news to Batto.

Redi Nenda went to Walawwe Hamine's place to distribute their clothes. She put the stack of clothes on the floor and sat on the small stool that was brought by Walawwe Hamine. Then she started to hand over the clean and ironed clothes one by one to Walawwe Hamine. While counting the number of clothes she spoke to Redi Nenda; "I heard, you have got flood aid," Hamine asked Redi Nenda.

"Yes, Hamine."

"Now they collect details of damaged houses due to flood to give aids. Your house was also damaged, was'nt it?" she asked.

"Yes Hamine, where do they write, Hamine?"

"Why, you don't know? Everyone is writing details at *Ralahami*'s."

"Oh, we did not know. By now it might be over then," Redi Nenda asked.

"I think, that is not over yet," Walawwe Hamine said.

Batto left home to meet *Ralahami*, the Grama Sewaka, next day morning. *Ralahami* was at home. Batto took the kerchief from his shoulder to his hand and started to speak to *Ralahami* with great reverence.

"*Ralahami*!"

"Yes, Batto, why?"

"I came to know that aid is given to damaged houses from flood. Our house also got damaged". He submitted his matter very obediently before *Ralahami*.

"Are you here to take aid for the house you live in?"

"Yes, *Ralahami*."

"But that house does not belong to you, isn't it, though you are living there."

"But, *Ralahami*, it was such a loss to us," replied Batto in a pleading tone. We are the victims."

"What can I do about it, Batto?"

"Once the house we live in, gets affected severely from flood, aid should be given to me," his tone became even more pleading.

"I don't know about it Batto, I told you about the law imposed by the government, if you want, you may bring a letter from your landlord that you're occupying his house."

"Please, *Ralahami*, try to get me some aid somehow," requested Batto as he had nothing much to do.

That evening, Batto went to meet Mahagedara *Ralahami*. He was at home.

"Batto, what made you come this way?" asked *Ralahami*.

"Government is giving aid to damaged houses from flood. *Ralahami* told me to bring a letter from you to claim it."

"What should I mention in the letter?"

"You only need to mention that we are occupying your house. That's more than enough," Batto said.

"Batto, you may stay in my house as long as you want. But I cannot give you a letter confirming it. It would result in you claiming for its ownership one day. And I will one day have to bear its loss," replied Mahagedara *Ralahami*.

"Oh sir! We have no such intention, sir. It was upon *Ralahami*'s request that I came here," pleaded Batto again

"The house is yours. We will never claim its ownership, Sir."

Batto returned home empty handed.

"If you are badly in need of aid, you may go and meet *Disapathituma*, with a letter," said the *Grama Sewaka Ralahami* when Batto went to meet him in the evening. But Batto knew that it would be such a difficult task and he had no confidence to act on his advice.

He had no courage to go and meet *Disapathituma*, the Government Agent at Matara.

"It is not good to delay this. You should go and meet *Disapathituma* tomorrow itself," said Redi Nenda. He was encouraged by the pestering of the other family members at home.

Batto wore a shirt tied at the shoulder with a thread and left early for Matara the next morning. There was a towel on his shoulder. All the clothes he used to wear were ones among the collected from the houses in the village for washing. He walked up to Kadduwa and by the time he reached Kadduwa, the bus had already left for Matara. Therefore, he had to wait at Kadduwa for two-three hours until the next bus arrived. He reached Matara by bus and decided to walk up to the *Kachcheri* where *Disapathituma* had his office, but had no courage to do so. He also felt that meeting *Disapathituma* too would be a difficult task. He was now reluctant to go meet *Disapathituma* and explain his concern to him. Moreover he thought it would have been better if he had stayed back looking into his day to day work of washing clothes. He thought that he came there for a futile task and stopped for a few seconds at the bus stand.

He again convinced himself and started stepping slowly towards the Kachcheri from the bus-stand. He was sweating due to fatigue. He saw the grandeur of the Kachcheri building and other tall buildings at a distance. He got a petition written by paying fifty cents and walked towards *Disapathituma*'s office. By now he had gathered some courage.

He was waiting at the door for sometime until *Arachchi* give him a chance to enter the office. He felt that he moved automatically in the office. He felt as if he had entered a new world that did not belong to him.

When he entered the office a serious looking middle aged gentleman was sitting on his chair at the table and writing something. Batto thought he would be the *Disapathituma*. A fan was spinning above his head. His heart started to thump fast. He thought that he would be chased right away as the prescence of a low caste, washerman-*Radawa* in the honorable *Disapathituma*'s room would be considered as something bad. His legs started to wobble.

Batto took the towel which was on his shoulder on to his hand to show his respect. He was waiting obediently and patiently until *Disapathituma* lifted his head. He was holding the petition in his right hand. *Disapathituma* lifted his head after a while and looked at him.

"Yes, why?" asked *Disapathituma*. He was getting ready to listen to his problem, Batto thought.

"Sir, due to flood… due to flood…," Batto started to smatter. He could not speak properly. No words came to his mouth.

"Ok, ok, what happened?" asked *Disapathituma*.

"Sir, our house got flooded. A large part of it got damaged. They say it's difficult to pay any compensation for the damage," said Batto while handing him over the petition.

Disapathituma read the petition.

"Doesn't the house belong to you?"

"No sir."

"Have you got a letter from the landlord?"

"No sir."

"I am sorry, it is impossible to give you any aid without a letter from the landlord though you are living there." *Disapathituma* pronounced his verdict and Batto turned back accepting his verdict obediently.

His defeat, he accepted as something inevitable and as something that he deserves.That was the house he and his family actually lived in all throughout their life. It was seriously damaged by flood. Although there was a Government move to give aids for damaged houses in the village, he could not get any compensation. That was the sad side of the law imposed in the village. Batto thought. "Where is justice? I spent all my money to come here, but I have to go home empty-handed. Everything was made in vain." This was another defeat for him like all other times. That is one hereditary thing for their people, he thought. Therefore, it was no shock to him, as usual.

18

Though, Samy was the oldest in the family, he behaved as if he was not a part of their family. He came home once or twice a month. He was really busy at Podi Mahattaya's place.

Troubles started to invade them unexpectedly one after the other.

That evening, Peter who worked in Podi Mahattaya's boutique came running towards the house and jumped over the stile.

"Samy has been taken by the police," he said to Redi Nenda who was in the courtyard.

"For what?" asked Redi Nenda in a perturbed tone.

"Police has raided Podi Mahattaya's *Kasippu Wadiya*," said Peter and ran away.

"Oh My God! What a crime! Why was Samy taken by the Police?" Redi Nenda started to lament. Babi who was inside the house heard this and came out. Batto too came hearing her shout.

"What's wrong?"

"*Ayya* has been taken to the police," replied Babi looking at Batto.

"Why is that?" asked Batto.

"They have raided Podi Mahattaya's *Kasippu*, it seems," she explained.

"Get dressed quickly to go to the police," Redi Nenda urged Batto while she wass still crying.

"Be patient, but what can we do if we go to the police? Better we go and meet Podi Mahattaya instead. He will tell what we should do," said Batto.

"Do whatever you can," Redi Nenda pleaded.

"Podi Mahattaya is involved in the *Kasippu* business, but poor Samy has been taken to the police for Podi Mahattaya's business. What a law!" said Batto in a fed-up tone to himself.

"Do whatever you can, do quickly," Redi Nenda said again.

Batto walked towards the stile through the courtyard to go meet Podi Mahattaya. But at the same moment Podi Mahattaya came fast riding a bicycle and stopped at the stile by the side of the tar road. Batto Vidane walked over to Podi Mahattaya.

"Batto...," he spoke while sitting on the bicycle itself placing one leg on the ground.

"Batto, you should not be scared. I'll take care of the whole matter. I'll do everything possible to get him released. I'll take revenge from whoever who tipped off the police," said Podi Mahattaya angrily.

Samy was released the next day. That day he came home straightaway before going to Podi Mahattaya's place.

"Podi Mahattaya rescued me on bail. Told me to come to court on the tenth of next month. That is all." Samy said to the others.

"Is it ok to work under Podi Mahattaya. If something bad happens will he look after everything?" asked Redi Nenda after hearing Samy's story.

Batto didn't say anything, but his face had a look of disapproval. He knew that even at home he did not have the ability to speak anything against Podi Mahattaya. Even others in the family knew that. That is why he remained silent like a rat at such moments.

The case against Podi Mahattaya's *Kasippu* was heard in the Matara Court. Samy pleaded guilty before the courts and he was fined fifty rupees. Podi Mahattaya paid the fine and released him. Everything was over in one day.

Though the court case was finished, the event was not finished. In fact it was the beginning of a series of troublesome events.

Podi Mahattaya believed that the tip off to the police about his *Kasippu* business was given by Siripala.

"I will not allow him to live," said Podi Mahattaya one day where he was drunk at his boutique.

Siripala was a new young man who had started a new boutique in the same village. Podi Mahattaya was a middle-aged man who had three four businesses. But more people were attracted to Siripala's boutique as most of the latest grocery was available at his boutique. His boutique was located close to the Cooperative outlet. "The goods that were brought to the Cooperative shop, went to Siripala's boutique in the evening," some people in the village said. Some items that were kept for sale in the cooperative shop were available in his shop too.

"He does not know who I am. Unless he keeps quiet when cheating goods from the cooperative shop, why he interfere in my work?" Podi Mahattaya challenged Siripala.

Earlier the grudge between Podi Mahattaya and Siripala did not surface and was kept like a fire under ashes. But after a few months, it aggravated and the villagers sensed an impending brawl between them. At any time there will be an open fight like an open fire, all the villagers said.

Siripala came on a bicycle and stopped at the stile of Batto's house. Batto was in the courtyard tying up a string between two coconut trees to put clothes to dry up in the sun.

"Batto, come here! Need to tell you something."

"What sir?" asked Batto coming towards Siripala.

"You may ask Samy to come back home before things get worse"

"Why is that sir?"

"Do you know that Podi Mahattaya is keeping him under his arm as a pawn."

"Oh sir, he won't listen to us. He even comes home rarely. Even though, he comes, he does not listen to whatever we tell." Batto continued as if he had accepted the defeat.

"I don't know about it and don't let me repeat this for he'll ultimately be in trouble."

"What Siripala Mahattaya telling is true. Podi Mahattaya keeps him under his arms not because he's concerned about my son. He's using him as a guinea pig," replied Redi Nenda hearing the story and replied before the other members of the family.

"What can we do, for he's too stubborn," said Batto in his usual calm tone.

Just as the villagers predicted, Podi Mahattaya's affiliates had threatened Siripala while he was on his way to the paddy field. Siripala too never surrendered. The argument developed into a brawl and Siripala got injured. Podi Mahattaya's assistants too got severely injured. Samy, and another assistant also got injured.

When Batto heard that Samy was admitted to the hospital, he started blaming Podi Mahattaya. That is because he had come to a point where he could not bear the pressure any more. Otherwise they usually didn't blame anyone in the village. "Let him do whatever he wants, I don't care a thing," said Batto and he walked into the house from the verandah.

Redi Nenda went to see Samy in the hospital the next day along with Babi. They had to face big trouble on their way to the hospital. They went to Kadduwa by foot and had to wait a long time there until a bus arrived. They got on to the bus. There were others in the bus. They were also going to the hospital to see injured Siripala.

Babi made sure that Redi Nenda was seated near the window as she always felt nauseous when she used to travels in a bus. Babi was seated next to Redi Nenda. If Redi Nenda felt like vomiting she could put her head out of the window and relieve herself. Redi Nenda was trying to fall asleep on the seat. Babi saw that her mother was struggling to fall asleep in the bus to avoid vomiting. Redi Nenda cuddled up on the seat and developed a slight hiccup too. Her eyes were closed uncertainly. Her head was bent towards the floor. She did not raise her head because if by any chance she looked out, giddiness could come and vomiting could happen.

The bus was speeding fast towards Matara. Time to time Redi Nenda choked on her seat. Babi thought that she was about to vomit. She looked around in fear. So far no one in the bus knew about the change in Redi Nenda's behavior. Redi Nenda could not control her pressure. Babi turned her head and looked around. Still no one was paying attention to them. For a moment Babi was happy. But finally Redi Nenda's ability to keep up the pressure was lost.

She at once started to vomit out of the window. The whole bus became impatient at once. Windows behind the seats where Redi Nenda and Babi were sitting were closed quickly.

Babi turned her head and looked at the seat at the back where she heard one telling, "This is such a filth, put your head outside the window and vomit, will you." It was one of Siripala's uncles who was sitting in the seat behind them. Babi understood the reason of him speaking against her mother vomiting.

Babi felt so uneasy. People in the bus were giving Redi Nenda a disgusting look. Babi looked at her mother and bent her head down to the floor. Her vomiting stopped for a moment.

Redi Nenda started to vomit again faster than before and people were looking at her with a disgusting look. The bus was speeding fast. People did not take that as a strange thing. Vomiting was a common thing for rural people when they go in buses. However, Babi was feeling uneasy and looked around.

A few drops of saliva were carried away by the wind and dropped at the seat where Siripala's uncle was sitting. With that, Siripala's uncle and the other person sitting on the seat rose from their seats.

"You bastard, Radavas! Why can't you stay at home, you sinners! Your dirt is all over our bodies." Siripala's uncle's voice was loud. Some of the other passengers in the bus joined Siripala's uncle.

"Why can't you vomit without causing us any trouble? Cant you put your head out of the window," said another passenger.

Redi Nenda closed her eyes and curled up on the seat as a snail that goes into its shell. Babi was too angry about the comment made by Siripala's uncle. He was also on his way to the hospital to see Siripala who was also a casualty from the incident that happened with Samy. Babi could understand why Siripala's uncle spoke so angrily. But Babi was helpless and she could do nothing at that moment and had to control her anger until they reached Matara. Though there were some of the passengers who knew that they belonged to Rada caste and washing clothes of others, Babi as well as the others of her family could not bear if someone commented anything referring to their caste. But she was not in a position to avoid such a situation. She was helpless; she could not react to them by any means.

Injured Samy, Podi Mahattaya's other assistant and Sripala were admitted in the same ward in the hospital. Both Samy and Podi Mahattaya's other assistant were badly injured.

Samy returned home after two weeks in the hospital. The following week, Samy stayed at home with his family.

"I go to work for Podi Mahattaya," one day Samy said to his mother. All the others were against his decision.

"Can't you learn a lesson out of all these, Samy? Don't you like to stay at home and help us with our washing business even now?" Batto asked.

"I can't do it. I will do something else. What can I get by washing clothes of others?" replied Samy angrily.

Batto never talked about it thereafter. From the second week, Samy returned to work in Podi Mahattaya's *Kasippu Wadiya*.

19

"Cannot believe how the prices of things go up. Last month a packet of blue was one twenty cents. Now it has gone up to one forty cents. Don't know from where we should earn money to buy all these." Darkness in the evening came to invade Batto's house when he came across the stile of the fence. Redi Nenda heard what Batto said about the price of blue that they used to whiten clothes.

"Not only blue, price of soda too went up last month," replied Redi Nenda coming to the verandah from the inside of the house.

"Yes, prices of everything are going up. To whom should we complain? But we should continue our job. If we don't do this, we will not have anything to eat," said Batto while sitting on the bed in the verandah. The bed made a creaky *kiri-kiri* noise.

Redi Nenda had once informed Batto that they didn't get sufficient rice like in the earlier days from the houses they provided their washing service to.

"All these happen to poor us," said Redi Nenda. "From one side prices of blue and soda are going up, from the other side return for washed clothes is going down," said Redi Nenda.

Redi Nenda now didn't get things that she used to get sometime ago from a *Kotahalu Magula*, when a girl attained her age. She used to get the girl's clothes and all her jewellery that she was wearing at the time she attained her maturity age. That was a right of the Rada caste of the village. But nowadays she did not get it. Villagers neglected that custom.

"*Nende*, please don't get angry with me. The girl was not wearing any gold when she attained age," the mother of the girl usually told Redi Nenda. Redi Nenda knew that it was not true. Most of the villagers were in the habit of removing jewellery from the girl's ears as she neared the age of puberty. They did it because, if jewellery remains on the body, they would have to give them away to Redi Nenda. So now, Redi Nenda lost the opportunity of getting such jewellery too.

Both Redi Nenda and Babi were wearing earrings they got from such girls *at Kotahalu Magula*. Now, they got some food stuff sufficient for four-five days and some money instead.

Everything they received from a *Kotahalu Magula* transformed gradually into money. In the same way most of the other customs had also changed.

Earlier, Batto's family used to get paddy after the havesting period of the villagers for their service. It was sufficient for them to survive for a season, if they used it efficiently. Now, that practice had also been replaced by money. Only a few traditional houses in the village still gave them paddy for their washing service. Others now gave them a few bucks, but the loss from this transition was for Batto's family. In a changing world where everything was converting into money, Batto and the rest of the family had to earn a lot of money for all their needs.

The news of a wedding of a son of one of the nobles in the village spread across the village. With that news both Redi Nenda and Batto were awaken with new courage. Because they knew that they could get something worth from them. Just as Batto had expected one evening Nelligoda Bala Mahattaya came to see him at his place.

"Batto, I need the *Wiyana* ready by the twenty-fourth evening." It was customary for them to tie up pieces of white cloth under the roof of the house to form a cloth ceiling when any function was to take place in any house in the village. That cloth ceiling was called *Wiyana*. "The wedding is on the twenty-fifth. Twenty-sixth is the home-coming ceremony and you should be there to perform your customs from our side," Nelligoda Bala Mahattaya explained everything.

They wanted twelve long white pieces of cloth to install the *Wiyana*. Batto collected some white cloth pieces brought from the houses to be washed. He went to Nelligoda Bala Mahattaya's place in the evening on that particular day along with Addin and the white cloth pieces. Addin was an expert in tying *Wiyana*.

Both Batto and Redi Nenda went for the home-coming of Nelligoda Bala Mahattaya's house to perform customs. It was Batto who spread a white cloth as a *Pawada* on the floor at the door step for the bride's party as it was the custom. That custom has to be done by Batto's family. Batto liked to spread the *Pawada* before people gathered at the wedding house. It was a pride for him, he thought. The young couple with the bride's relatives walked on the *Pawada*, and they kept their first step on it by dropping a currency note on it. Once the couple and the party passed the *Pawada*, Batto took the currency note dropped on the cloth and tucked it in his waist. He could identify the type of the note by its colour. It was the best part of the wedding for him he thought.

When all the relatiives took their seats at the rich lunch table of the home-coming ceremony, Batto also got a special place at the corner of the same table as it was customary to invite him to the table. Though, his presence was customary at the table, the chair reserved for him was smaller than the other chairs for when he enjoys food with others, everyone can easily recognise Batto as the man who washes clothes for this family.

At the end of the home-coming ceremony in the evening after removing the *Wiyanas*, Batto was given some money for arranging the *Wiyanas*. Batto simply did not need to think whether that money was sufficient to wash the clothes used for the Wiyana as this was a traditional duty performed by people of his clan for centuries. He performed such tasks quietely keeping in mind that he was bound to do them. Redi Nenda also got some extra portion of food that was left over after the ceremony. She took it home as if she was given a treasure for she knew that Babi and Addin too were awaiting that food. They got to eat something tasty only on such days.

Redi Nenda and Batto were quite hopeful of the help extended by Addin to the family. He started going for manual labour at some neighbouring houses and earned a few bucks at the end of the day. He spent that money on expenses at home and Redi Nenda considered it a big relief for their family.

"He has always been attached to us," uttered Batto.

Addin preferred to do manual labour at neighbouring houses, as he was given something to eat for lunch from those houses. That was a part of the return for doing labour. Addin knew that his mother could not give him a good meal at home. Addin being a hefty young man did not get sufficient food to quench his hunger at home. Therefore, he knew that he was sure to get something better for lunch from houses where he rendered his labour.

Batto and Redi Nenda too did not stop him for doing such work, for it helped them ease the burden at home. Every time Redi Nenda thought Addin's contribution helped raise their family. She suffered on the noncontributory living by Samy. She had more confidence on Addin.

After a long hearing of two-years, the court case of Siripala and Samy ended with Samy being imprisoned for two years. That was a defeat for Podi Mahattaya.

"Don't be afraid, I will take care of your family," said Podi Mahattaya to Batto when he visited Batto's place on the day Samy was convicted. He was on the bicycle with his one leg on the stile of the fence, when he spoke with Batto. Redi Nenda was little away from them.

"But sir, we won't be able to see him for two years," coming closer to them replied Redi Nenda wiping off her tears with his palm.

"If possible, I'll try to get him released before his term ends". Even though Samy got released before two years Batto knew that it was not for the sympathy of their family, but for his own benefit. He wanted Samy to look after his Kasippu business. He could not run the business without Samy. But Batto could not spell out those emotions before anyone. So he had to hide all these emotions in his mind. This habit was inherited from his ancesters. Though Podi Mahattaya said that he would help the family, he never kept his word. Though Samy did not do any considerable help for the family earlier, once Podi Mahattaya told them that he would help them, they expected something or the other for their day-to-day existence.

"All are selfish and concerned about their own benefit," said Addin.

"Yeah, that's how things happen; no one cares for the others. Everyone runs for their own benefit," Batto replied.

Batto lost the helping hand he received from Addin for washing clothes as he was now going to work at neighbouring houses. Therefore, the washing process was entirely done by Batto and Redi Nenda. It was Babi who performed the other household chores and all the work in the kitchen fell on Babi's shoulder. Babi kept something ready to eat when they returned home after work from the river. They ate whatever was available, for what they wanted was something to swallow to fulfill their hunger. They only wanted to eat something to pass the meal time. They did not bother about the taste or the nourishment of what they ate.

20

"*Appochchi*, wouldn't it be good if we seek permission from Mahagedara *Ralahami*, to grow some maniocs on this land, there's so much of land vacant. I can do the planting." One day while they were waiting for their dinner to be served Addin asked Batto. Addin was sitting on the string bed at the corner of the verandah. Batto was also sitting bent on the bed at the other corner of the verandah. Batto heard what Addin said and turned to look at him. Batto's eyes could still see in dark, so he could see Addin sitting on the bed at the other corner. With Batto's movement the string bed made a *kiri-kiri* kind of noise. It was nearing full moon day hence there was moonlight falling on a part of the courtyard. Light came across the door from the bottle lamp inside the house and illuminated a part of the verandah. That beam of light spread to the courtyard through the verandah.

"It is a good idea. But I will have to first ask him. I am scared that he might chase us from this place too if we go to ask for such a favour. They will not allow us to grow anything on this land." Batto did not speak much, but he could see far ahead than the others.

However, Batto went to meet Mahagedara *Ralahami* that evening. He was at home. As he saw

Mahagedara *Ralahami*, Batto took the kerchief which was on his shoulder on to his hand. That happened automatically, because it was a custom that had to be followed by low caste people like Batto to show their respect. In addition he bent forward to show his regards and got behind *Ralahami*. Then as he was just about to open his mouth to speak,

"What brings you here, Batto?" *Ralahami* said breaking into the conversation before Batto.

"*Ralahami*, I came here to make a request to you," said Batto in a pleading manner. He bent forward again to show his respect to *Ralahami*.

"What is it?" asked Mahagedara *Ralahami*.

"*Ralahami*, I came here to ask if it is ok, if we plant a few manioc plants on your land where we live."

Mahgedara *Ralahami* heard him and pondered for a while looking up. Then he started to speak.

"M…m…m, if you plant manioc there ,the land will become wasted. So, let the land be as it is," Mahgedara *Ralahami* refused Batto's request.

Batto had no courage to go beyond his words. Batto had no such habit too.

"Any land gets wasted when you plant manioc," said one of *Raluhami*'s assistants who was listening to their conversation.

"Mahagedara *Ralahami* may have thought that as there are two boys for us we were trying to take the ownership of the land," said Redi Nenda after listening to the story at home. "I also thought the same thing." Batto added to his wife's reply.

"And what right has the other man got to support *Ralahami*? Why did he join the discussion you had, what is the use?" Redi Nenda blamed the other man.

"It is no point blaming anyone. This is our destiny," Batto said in a fed-up tone.

Addin who returned home after work in the evening said, "What's wrong in planting something on this bare land?" Redi Nenda had explained to Addin what happened when Batto met Mahagedara *Ralahami*.

Batto who was walking slowly in a lazy mood on the road, turned towards Podi Mahattaya's boutique. There was mud all over at the two sides of the road after the rain in the night. When he stepped in to the boutique avoiding mud on the ground, he saw a group of people looking at a notice pasted on the trunk of the big mango tree just opposite the boutique. He also joined them and tried to read the notice. It was a notice written by hand and pasted on the tree. He tried to understand the content of the notice.

The notice was about the distribution of a land called 'Nakanda' among landless villagers. He read the notice with difficulty and squatted in a corner of the boutique.

"It is a thick forest full of jackals. Can a human go live there?" said Haramanis taking the newspaper kept in between the two bottles of biscuits at the counter and sitting on the bench at the verandah.

"Not only that; it is a hillock. It's difficult to build any house there," said Podi Mahattaya joining the conversation. He was coming out from the boutique.

"But, for people like us, it would be a great asset as we have nothing," Piyadasa who was sitting on the same bench responsed.

"Whatever it is, I too should ask for a plot of land from there," turning his head towards the boutique, Batto said breaking the silence.

"If you leave the village, who would wash our clothes?" looking at him, Podi Mahattaya said in response to Batto's suggestion.

"This is also true," replied Haramanis lifting his head from the newspaper.

Batto who remained silent for a while, stopped chewing betel for a moment and spat a thick red betel saliva on the ground through the two fingers put on the mouth. It made a big red patch on the ground. Then he stepped on to the road.

"It is also true," responding to Podimahattaya's comment replied Haramanis lifting his face from the paper.

That day Batto returned home happily compared to the other days. His heart was filled with hope. Getting a plot of land from the Land Kachcheri would be the best victory ever for Batto. This was a new hope for someone like Batto who had experienced nothing but defeat his entire life.

He thought he's eligible enough to get a piece of land.

Being usually silent all the time, he spoke a lot at home that day. He spoke a lot with Redi Nenda, Addin and Babi. Sometimes he spoke with himself too.

"It is better you leave early tomorrow before *Gramasewaka Ralahami* leaves for any other work," said Redi Nenda.

When Batto went see *Gramasewaka Ralahami* who was responsible for the village administration, his presence at home was considered lucky by him. *Ralahami* wrote down all the information necessary, asking questions from Batto.

"*Ralahami*, I pray you to get us a plot of land," pleaded Batto before the *Gramasewaka Ralahami*.

"Ok, we'll see when *Disapathituma* comes for the Land Kachcheri to select people. When he asks questions, you have to respond," said Gramasewaka *Ralahami*.

The day Land Kachcheri was held, Batto went to the school early morning. It was where the Land Kachcheri was held. Addin was also with him. By the time he went to the school, some people had already come. They were idling there discussing different views they were having in the village.

"There are about eighty people waiting to get just twenty plots of land it seems," they were discussing.

By noon, *Gramasewaka Ralahami* came there and spread a table cloth on a table and made it ready for the inquiry. After a while, a jeep arrived at the school.

The officer who was seated in the front seat of the jeep wore a pair of spectacles and had a serious look. From the way he behaved, everyone got to know that he was the *Disapathituma*. When he got off from the vehicle and was coming towards the school building all made way for him with utmost respect. *Gramasewaka Ralahami* walked towards him and welcomed the *Disapathituma*. Another officer who was walking alongside him was carrying a bundle of files.

Disapathituma took his seat. *Gramasewaka Ralahami* and the assistant who was carrying files sat on either side of him. All those who were gathered in the school premises flocked around them.

"Silence!" *Gramasewaka Ralahami* got up from his seat and pushed he crowd back. Batto was standing a little away from the crowd and Addin was behind him. Batto was in a sarong with a shawl over the shoulder. His upper body was naked.

Gramasewaka Ralahami started calling out names one by one. *Disapathituma* was writing down the responses the villagers gave him for his questions on a big book which was spread on the table.

"Hewa Radage Batto!" his name was called and he walked slowly towards *Disapathituma* and stood in front of him. He took the shawl on his shoulder down to his left hand and shyly answered the questions raised by *Disapathituma*.

Disapathituma asked him many details such as his name, age, marital status, the number of children and whether the children were married. Batto answered all the questions.

"Your age?"

"About fifty years sir," repled Batto shyly.

"According to the birth date you mentioned you should be more than sixty, shouldn't you?" asked *Disapathituma*.

"Oh sir, I don't know sir. Am I so old?"

"You are too old to be entitled for this land"

"Oh sir, if that's so my son is here. Can you please give him a piece of land? We don't own a single inch of land."

"Who is he? Is that your son?"

"Yes sir," replied Addin and turned back. Addin was standing just behind him and he came forward shyly.

"Is this your own son?" asked *Disapathituma*.

"Yes sir," replied Batto in a pleading tone

"How old is he?"

Batto waited a little to answer. By the time Addin replied for the question. "Twenty three"

"Is he married?"

"Not yet sir," replied Batto.

"We don't give lands to unmarried. Only the married ones could apply for lands,"continued Disapathituma.

"So, sir, won't we get any land at all?" asked Batto with unbearable pain.

"How can you get it, you are too old and your son is still unmarried"

Gramasewaka Ralahami called out the next name.

Batto was feeling faint by now. He turned back with Addin and stopped only at the verandah of his house. Redi Nenda who was expecting their return appeared through the kitchen.

"What happened?" She asked while Batto and Addin settled on the string bed at the verandah.

Batto did not utter a word. He sat on the bed bending forward and put two hands around his two knees.

"We didn't get any land," replied Addin instead of Batto.

"Why is that? Is it because they thought that we have lands?" asked Redi Nenda.

"No, because father is too old and I am not married," Addin continued.

"Hmmm…" replied Redi Nenda and walked inside the house as a snake going towards its den.

21

Gramasewaka Ralahami parked his bicycle at the stile and stepped into Batto's courtyard. He peeped in to the house. No one was there to be seen. He cleared his throat. With that sound Babi came to the verandah and she recognised the *Gramasewaka Ralahami* who was still at the courtyard.

"Where's your *Appochchi*?" asked *Ralahami* from Babi.

"He is there; at that side." Babi replied directing her hand to the backside of the house.

"Tell him that I am here."

Babi ran to the backyard and called out to her father loudly. "*Appochchi*! *Ralahami* has come."

Batto came to the front side of the courtyard. Soon he saw *Ralahami* and stretched down his sarong which was always folded up in two. That was done by him traditionly to show his regards to *Ralahami*.

"Batto, I came here for an important matter." "What's it, *Ralahami*?" Batto asked.

"You send your *Kella* to our place for a few days. The servant girl has gone and she did not return; my wife is also unable to do the chores on her own."

"*Ralahami*, she's the only one who looks after at home," said Batto. "Anyway, when my wife returns home I will discuss the matter with her and send her to your place." Though Batto was reluctant to send her to *Ralahami*'s place he couldn't refuse his request straight away. He could not go against *Ralahami* and he had to do what *Ralahami* asked.

"Don't worry. There's not much of work. She's only got to take care of my little one. She would be comfortable there with food and everything," said *Ralahami*.

"Oh, no, *Appochchi*, I won't go anywhere," said Babi after *Ralahami* left. She started crying.

"How can we send her, she's the only one at our place to do the chores," said Redi Nenda when she returned home in the evening. She was angry.

"But, what can we do? What if he gets angry with us? After all, he's an influential man in the village,we need him for everything and if he gets angry over a simple matter of this nature, it would be difficult for us to survive in this village," Batto said.

"This is such a funny deal. As if we have brought up our children to donate for their sake," said Redi Nenda angrily.

"Keep your mouth shut, woman. What if he gets to know what you said? He can do anything to us. After all he is the *Ralahami* in this village," said Batto. He wanted to balance everything.

The next day evening, Redi Nenda accompanied Babi to *Ralahami*'s place. *Ralahami*'s wife treated Redi Nenda well.

That night the house without Babi was engulfed with loneliness. Everyone was sad. Redi Nenda didn't take her dinner as she could not convince herself that Babi was no more in the house. She could not bear the absence of Babi at home.

"The house looks empty and lonely without her in one day," Batto who was sitting on the string bed, didn't want anyone to hear what he said.

But Addin who was coming towards the verandah, heard what Batto said. Addin walked to the other corner of the verandah and sat on the other bed. It made a kiri-kiri sound when he sat on it. Hearing that sound Batto looked at him. He saw the dark naked upper part of the body of Addin in the darkness.

"*Appochchi*, you should have stopped *Akka* from going there," Addin responded to his father.

"How can I do it? Do you think we would have any solace if *Ralahami* gets angry with us?" Addin had no answer for Batto's question. Therefore, he remained silent.

After Babi went to *Gramasewaka Ralahami*'s place Redi Nenda had to do all the household chores that were done earlier by Babi. So she had to attend to all cooking activities by herself. She had to arrange *Wellawa* and put fire time to time. She had to get up early in the morning take the stack of clothes with Batto to the ferry for washing. In the afternoon she had to take washed clothes for distribution among the houses. Without Babi for everything, Redi Nenda had to make a very big effort. However she did everything without any hesitation.

Addin left home early morning to earn a few bucks. He used to come back home late in the evening. Then he had time only to help his mother by ironing clothes in the evening. He could not do anything other than that. Therefore, both Redi Nenda and Batto had to shoulder all the work at home patiently.

Day by day, the amount they had to spend on soap, soda, and fabric blue, in addition to day to day needs of the family, increased and they wanted more money for their expenses too. But they had no courage to ask for more money from the houses they served for cleaning clothes. Though, Addin went out for manual labour almost every day, which too was not sufficient to cover their expenses as he got only a small payment for his manual labour at the neighbouring houses.

While Redi Nenda, Addin and Batto were gradually becoming exhausted with their work, Babi got a new lease of life as she was given sufficient food to eat at *Ralahami*'s place. Though she looked frail earlier, she had become quite good looking. She used to come home from time to time to see her parents. *Ralahami* too treated them well. Whenever, Redi Nenda went to *Ralahami*'s place she was given some rice, a coconut or a jackfruit and she considered it a grand treat.

"I'm at least happy that she gets something to eat and dress there," said Redi Nenda one day while she was talking to Batto at their verandah after dinner.

"It is ok, if we don't get anything as long as she's happy," said Batto.

Only Batto was available at home when Babi came home that day. On other days she usually came home to see her parents and brother. But that day she came home not to see her family members but for a different purpose.

There was restlessness on her face that was never seen before. Babi looked impatient. She walked up to the kitchen and again walked back from kitchen to the verandah several times. She became even more impatient as her mother was not around.

"*Appochchi*, where's *Amma*," she asked from Batto. Even in her tone there was restlessness.

"She has taken the clothes to distribute. She will come in a while. What's wrong" asked Batto from Babi. He sensed the excitement appearing in Babi's face.

"No, nothing; will she come soon?"

"She might; she didn't go that far. She took only a few clothes with her as she could not iron all the clothes."

When Redi Nenda returned home Babi followed her to the kitchen. Uneasyness shown in Babi's behavior was sensed by Redi Nenda.

"You look weird today?" asked Redi Nenda as she could not tolerate Babi's unease.

"I can't go to *Ralahami*'s place," said Babi in an awkward manner. Redi Nenda felt that there could be something wrong.

"Why is that? All of a sudden, you were better off there, weren't you?"

"There's nothing, but I cannot go there," said Babi again.

"It is not good to say so. *Ralahami* will get angry with us. Then we could not live in this village," said Redi Nenda.

"I can't go. I was anyway taken there only for a few days. It has been a lot of months now," said Babi.

"It is not good to leave the place without informing them. You should have told them. It is not good to stay here all of a sudden."

"Ok, then; why don't you accompany me. Then I can plead him to release me from work and come," Babi pleaded before her mother.

"I can't go now, this evening. What actually has happened to you? You were good there and what made this change?" asked Redi Nenda.

"Nothing has happened to me. But I can't stay there."

"Did they hit you or scold you? Why do you want to come home soon?"

"I don't know. I can't stay there. I need to come home," said Babi.

"Here, did you hear what Babi said? She says she can't stay at *Ralahami*'s place," Redi Nenda said in a tone that could be clear enough for Batto to hear. Batto was making a string to put clothes to dry out in the sun, at the courtyard. Some of the strings were too old and those were to be replaced with new strings. So he was making those strings.

"Why is that? Aren't you better off there?" Batto asked Babi seriously.

"I can't stay there, I need to come home," replied Babi looking at him.

"Now, if you go tell *Ralahami* that you need to come home, he will think that we have brainwashed you to do it when you came here. If you can't stay there, *Amma* will come take you in a few days," said Batto patiently.

"Ok, I will bring you home in another few days. You may go now," said Babi's mother decisively.

"If you won't come, I will wait for about a week and come home by myself," said Babi and stepped on to the courtyard to leave for *Gramasewaka Ralahami's* place.

"You may go now; it is not good to make them our foes. After all, we didn't send you there willingly," said Batto to Babi when she was about to leave, with suppressed sympathy in his heart. "The girl doesn't like to stay at *Ralahami's* place," said Batto to Redi Nenda that night after dinner at the verandah.

"She may have found it difficult with *Ralahami's* wife. She must be wicked," said Redi Nenda doubtfully.

"Didn't she tell the reason?"

"No," said Redi Nenda.

"It is better if you could bring her home in two or three days," finally Batto said to Redi Nenda.

That day Addin came out of the house early and crossed the stile to go to find some day's labour. One bird at a bush nearby flew away crying. At once, his eye caught a white paper which was pasted on the bark of the Areca nut tree little away from the stile. He got closer to the tree and saw that something was written on it.

"*Ralahami*-Babi-illegal wife," Addin could no longer read it. His eyes turned blur. He tore off that paper from the tree and chopped it in his palm. He turned back and jumped over the stile and stepped onto the courtyard like a madman.

Batto, who had just woken up and entered the courtyard, saw Addin jump over the stile.

"What's up?" Batto saw the change in Addin's behaviour and asked at once.

"What…? Here, published wild papers," He said loudly with angry and thrust the crushed paper he had in his hand towards Batto. Batto could not understand properly what it is. He picked the crushed paper and unfolded it slowly. He read it with difficulty. While he was reading, he started to sweat from his head to toe. His heart started to burn like a fire in blaze. Batto was a man who considered everything patiently like a big rock not moving, but here his patience was smashed with this news like a water drop fell on a rock.

He remembered how Babi came home a few days ago, and how she refused to go back to *Ralahami's* place, and how she agreed to go back again after a lot of pestering.

Batto's house looked morbid. Everyone was uncertain and impatient. Addin started blaming *Ralahami* and his wife.

Redi Nenda went to *Ralahami's* place to bring Babi back home. She got thoroughly scolded by *Ralahami* and his wife.

"When your people are here, it brings chaos and bad reputation to us. Now we can't live here," *Ralahami* said.

"Though she pretends like an ascetic, she's so playful. How do we know?" said *Ralahami*'s wife.

Redi Nenada didn't utter a word nor was she allowed to open her mouth.

"When we pity them, it is a disaster for ourself," said *Ralahami*.

"She was playing around with all the men who used to come here and now that she's pregnant, why should my husband be blamed for that? We ourself did the wrong thing." *Ralahami*'s wife cried angrily.

Redi Nenda felt as if her body was in a blaze. Everything has gone wrong. According to them, the girl was at fault. She couldn't really figure out the authenticity of her claim. She became helpless in front of all those accusations and came out from *Ralahami*'s kitchen and stepped out into the garden with Babi to go back home.

Redi Nenda got the lead. Babi was sobbing while hugging her bundle of clothes to her mouth. She followed her mother. Her head was bent towards the floor. None of them lifted their heads until they reached their home.

Babi stepped in to the house and stopped in the kitchen. Redi Nenada stepped on to the verandah and stopped. When they came there, Batto was sitting on the bed in the verandah facing the courtyard.

He saw his wife escorting her daughter into the

house. Though he saw Babi coming he did not utter a word. He did not want to speak even to Redi Nenda.

Babi was crying in a corner of the kitchen. Addin was not at home at that time. Redi Nenda came to the kitchen where Babi was crying.

"Babi, you've got to tell me the truth. What happened to you?" Redi Nenda asked Babi. She was silent. Instead she was crying continuously.

"What did Hamine said that you're pregnant?" Redi Nenda asked again.

She cried continuously and did not speak.

"Tell me, tell me the truth. Tell me whether that story is correct or not," Redi Nenda pestered her.

But Babi never uttered a word.

"Tell, tell me the truth," pestered Redi Nenda again and again

But Babi continued to cry incessantly.

"Babi, tell me the truth, is that true?"

"Yes," Babi nodded her head while crying. Redi Nenda's body started to burn again. But, she knew it was useless worrying over it now.

"Then, who committed this crime? Was it anyone who used to come there?"

Babi cried continuously. She did not speak.

"Tell me the truth, who is that man?"

"*Ralahami*," whispered Babi crying. It was a broken and weak sound.

"*Ralahami?*" Redi Nenda repeated it.

"Yes."

"How dare he speak to me that way after doing all this," Redi Nenda spoke angrily.

"Yes," Babi replied in a weaker sound.

"Since when?"

"Three months," she whispered again.

'Now that everything has happened. There's nothing left to be done. Babi's life was ruined and the disgrace caused to the family was irretrievable,' Batto thought.

With time, Batto, Redi Nenda and Addin overcame the incident, but Babi did not step out of the house for a few months.

Babi gave birth to a boy. Redi Nenda thought that he looks exactly like *Gramasewaka Ralahami*. All at home loved the kid and he was growing up amidst love and care of all.

22

"Addin, can you bring a quarter a bottle of kerosene oil, and a quarter pound of sugar if you have got some money with you. There's no kerosene oil at home to light the lamp and there's no sugar for tomorrow morning," Redi Nenda asked Addin when he came home in the evening.

"I don't have any money, Amme," replied Addin.

Redi Nenda knew that Addin never lied. She knew that he always came forward to help the family when he had money with him.

"Didn't you find any work today?" Redi Nenda asked.

"What work? Unlike in the past, it's so difficult to get some work nowadays. I went everywhere in search of work. There was nothing. Don't know whether it's due to this drought," Addin's tone was full of grief and loss of hope.

"Then, where were you all this time?" asked Redi Nenda.

"I walked everywhere searching for some work until noon and finally ended up at Podi Mahattaya's place and I drank tea and ate lunch with the money I had."

"*Appochchi* might be there, on the other side."

"Ok, then tell him to bring those even on a loan, before night comes."

Their penury was increasing gradually. Though the money Addin used to bring was barely sufficient, that too was not coming now as there was no work in the village for manual labour. If the rain continued for a few more days, it would become even more difficult for him to find some work. If the river spilled over and flooded the low lands, Addin would not find any work. If he did not get work how could he find money? Not only that, when he didn't get work he didn't get to eat his lunch too from outside. Therefore, the whole family was in a state of danger.

Batto Vidane stepped out from Podi Mahattaya's boutique with a pound of soda and a packet of blue powder to come back home. He was feeling a little happy inside him due to a story he overheard there. When he was squatting aside at the verandah of Podi Mahattaya's boutique facing the road, he heard the story the others gathered there were discussing. The topic of the discussion was the forthcoming general election. That news made him happy with new expectations. When he recalled it his joyful feelings were renewed. Election was announced to be held soon.

"Mahagedara *Ralahami* is going to support the Dosthara Hamu it seems," said Sirisena enjoying a plain tea with a piece of jaggery. There were three people sitting on the bench at the verandah of the boutique. Another man was there standing at the edge of the verandah facing the road.

"He supports the Dosthara Hamu as he hopes to be the next Chairman of the Village Council, it seems," said Siyadoris who was standing there looking at the road.

"Yes, what only remains for *Ralahami* for now is to be the Chairman of the Village Council. If they have money, store filled paddy, servants for everything and what not. What else can they expect other than becoming the Chairman of the Village Council," said another one who had come there to buy keresone oil.

"Yes, other than the Temple and the Walawwa, most of the lands in the village are owned by none other than Mahagedara *Ralahami*, is'nt it? No other lands are needed, only Nalawila paddy field is enough. That is a bowl of rice, so fertile," said Siyadoris.

"Yes, you're correct. There's paddy everywhere in their house during the harvesting time," said another one.

Hearing that story Batto got a new idea that he too might be able to get a piece of land from *Ralahami* to cultivate. People in the village believed that Mahagedara *Ralahami* helped everyone in need. Therefore, he thought that he would not reject him if he asks for a paddy field. Batto and his people had rendered their service to him for generations.

Batto crossed the stile and walked silently towards the house. He sat on the string bed at the verandah and placed soda and the fabric blue powder brought in his hand on the bed itself. The bed as usual creaked under his weight.

Redi Nenda hearing Batto's arrival peeped towards the verandah.

"It is becoming so difficult and we can't go on like this. One pound of soda is one fifty, a packet of blue powder is five rupees, and a bar of soap is ninety cents. It's our bad luck for we cannot sustain our lives with a job," uttered Batto.

Branches of the trees around the house moved slowly with the wind. River beneath the tar road flowed quietly under the shade of trees. There was beauty in the quiet environment, Batto thought.

"People now don't give us clothes to wash. Those who gave us twenty-thirty pieces earlier now give only about seven-eight pieces. So we have to wait a number of weeks to collect clothes enough for a *Wellawa*. In good old days clothes brought from one house was enough for one *Wellawa*. We'll soon have to find another way to sustain ourselves," replied Redi Nenda approving what Batto said.

"I'm planning to get a piece of paddy land to work," Batto Vidane put his idea before his wife.

"From whom?" Redi Nenda asked.

"From Mahagedara *Ralahami*!"

"Does he have paddy lands to give if you asked for? Do you think he would give?"

"Let's ask and see," Batto finally said in confidence.

Mahagedara *Ralahami* was at home when Batto went to see him and he thought he was lucky as *Ralahami* was at home. Usually it was difficult to meet him at home on other days. *Ralahami* was in the garden. Batto put the towel on his fore-arm and bent towards him to pay his respect.

"Batto, what brings you here?" Once he saw Batto, *Ralahami* asked.

"I came to meet you," Batto murmured in a pleading tone.

"Why, any news of a wedding?" *Ralahami* asked again.

"No"

"Then, why, all of a sudden?"

"I came to ask whether you would be able to give me a plot of paddy field to work on," Batto put his idea before *Ralahami* with difficulty.

"A plot of paddy field?" *Ralahami* repeated it. "Can you work in a paddy field? Your people only know how to work with *Wellawa*, isn't it?"

"I can *Ralahami*. If one works hard what else cannot he do? Besides, Addin is also there for my help."

"Then, won't you continue your job?" *Ralahami* asked again.

"Oh! *Ralahami*, it has become so difficult to sustain our job nowadays. Soap and other things are so expensive and people also now don't give us their clothes to wash."

"But I highly doubt whether you would be able to do paddy farming."

"I can *Ralahami*. I'm capable of doing such work. You may see how I work," said Batto meekly.

"Ok, I will give you a piece of paddy field. It's a good furtile paddy field, once done by Diyonis. But he was a bit lazy. You work it on shared basis," *Ralahami* dictated his conditions.

"Ok *Ralahami*," Batto agreed. But he did not have any idea on working in shared basis.

"How many more times had I told Diyonis not to be lazy. But he didn't listen to me. Therefore, I was anyway planning to remove him from work. Then you may start working on it from the next season. It won't be that difficult for you. If you don't have money to buy pesticides and fertilizer I will buy it for you. I will also give seed paddy for you. "

"Oh, that's a great help." All the paddy fields owned by *Ralahami* were worked by farmers in the village on shared basis of the harvest. Batto Vidane had heard of that.

The deal was to get pesticides, seed paddy and fertilizer from *Ralahami*, and the yield would be equally divided between *Ralahami* and Batto after deducting the expenses made by *Ralahami* for pesticides, seed paddy and fertilizer. Batto thought that it would be easier that way.

That day he stepped out from *Ralahami*'s premises triumphantly. Both Addin and Redi Nenda were inquisitive to know more details of the paddy land. Batto talked too much on the paddy field at home.

Addin gave a very good helping for his father in working on the paddy field. It was a good relief for Batto. He treated the paddy well and enjoyed his new job rather than washing clothes. Fragrence of the wind came through the young paddy plantation was like a milky smell of a newly born child of the family. Batto liked to feel that fragrance. When paddy was ripe for harvest he protected it from birds and other wild animals. He chased away the parrots that came to eat ripe paddy with great enthusiasm. Addin too helped him with his work. All the members of the family were happy with the work in the paddy field.

When the paddy was ripened and ready for harvest, Batto went to see *Ralahami* to convey the message and get the dates for harvesting.

"Unlike Diyonis you've really worked hard," *Ralahami* commended the work that Batto had done in his paddy field. He was listening to what *Ralahami* said with a stupid smile.

Paddy was harvested, threshed and cleaned. They took another two days for cleaning paddy. Batto's heart was filled with happiness seeing the yield of paddy which was lying stacked on two borrowed big mats.

Ralahami came to see the yield everyday. Batto protected it with utmost care and spent the night protecting it from wild animals. Batto talked more on the paddy field and the yield at home.

In the evening Batto came there with a *Kuruniya*, the scale to measure the yield of paddy. There was a pile of gunny sacks on his shoulder. He looked happier than the other days. After a while, Mahagedara *Ralahami* too arrived there. He had a small note book in his hand. Batto, with Addin's help removed the hay cover which was kept on the stack of paddy closed with big mats. Then he sat at the edge of the stack of paddy and started measuring paddy with Kuruniya in to gunny sacks. *Ralahami* was watching it. Gunny sacks were filled one by one with paddy.

He got up from the big mat after finishing measuring the paddy. His body was wet with sweat. His legs were feeling numb as he was sitting for a long time to measure paddy yield. *Ralahami* started to count the number of paddy sacks one by one. Batto and Addin were only looking at it.

"Twelve paddy sacks, isn't it? Check whether it is correct?" said *Ralahami* after he finished counting the sacks.

Then, Batto too started counting one by one.

"Ok, *Ralahami*," said Batto after he finished counting.

Ralahami opened the note book in his hands and started to write something in it with his pencil.

"When twelve is divided by two, it's six sacks of paddy. That is for the owner's portion," *Ralahami* said with a grave tone. "Then you also get six paddy sacks, and out of that I will have to deduct for pesticides, fertilizer and seed paddy which counts upto hundred and thirty rupees. When that amount is deducted from paddy, you get only one sack of paddy, am I correct?" *Ralahami* finished the counting and closed the note book.

Batto was only listening to it silently. He thought that *Ralahami's* calculation is correct

With that, the paddy business was ended and *Ralahami's* cart was approaching. Batto and Addin loaded all the paddy into the cart and *Ralahami* too left with the cart.

Addin took the two mats rolled together onto his shoulder and took the empty *Kuruniya* into his right hand. Batto started to walk home silently with the one and only sack of paddy on his shoulder. He was bent forward a little with the weight of the sack of paddy. He placed the sack on the floor with a thundering noise and stretched himself on the string bed at the verandah. Addin who was coming behind him placed the two mats and the *Kuruniya* in the verandah and walked inside the house.

Redi Nenda came to the verandah from inside the house hearing the noise made from the falling of the sack of paddy on the floor.

"Is that all," asked Redi Nenda with a tone full of disappointment.

"Yes, one sack, sixteen *Kurunis* of paddy," Batto said. Redi Nenda looked at Batto's face.

"How many were there altogether?"

"Twelve sacks."

"Then, is this all we get for all the toil and hard work?""Yes, why not?" "Oh! No" said Redi Nenda utterly disappointed and bewildered. Batto never uttered a word about it that night though Redi Nenda was talking incessantly. Batto was silent the whole night. Addin seldomly joined his mother when she was talking.

23

"A meeting in support of representing the party," Addin heard the rough and broken announcement made on the loudspeaker. He was near the fence cleaning a timber pole with a knife. He lifted his head and looked at the road. A car was coming on the road from far and there was a loudspeaker fixed on its hood. He identified that the car belonged to a trader at Kadduwa. He also knew the news about the forthcoming General Election. Therefore, he understood what was announced through the loudspeaker. By that time election campaigns were becoming active even in the villages. Addin and others in the village knew that such propaganda was taking place all around the village. People talked about the parties contesting in the Election, everywhere from boutiques, work places and even in houses. There was huge enthusiasm among villagers that they had never experienced before on an election. Villagers were more interested in the forthcoming election activities and they were supporting different political parties.

"We don't want any political party, after all what purpose would it serve us," said Batto one evening to others at home. Batto had an understanding that if he was going to back one party it would harm his family.

He had that idea after hearing the discussions among villagers taking place at the boutique.

Two candidates from two famous families in the area representing Udaha Walawwa and Aluth Walawwa have come forward to contest for the election. It was Goring Hamu of Udaha Walawwa and Dosthara Hamu of Aluth Walawwa. Many in the village started supporting them. Batto and others in the family tried their best to remain impartial. But Samy was always with Podi Mahattaya and he had to follow him in the election campaign too.

"If Dosthara Hamu wins he is going to launch the Nilwala project it seems.," said someone who had come to Podi Mahattaya's boutique.

"Not only that, I also heard that he was going to acquire some lands from land owners and distribute those among poor people," said another. Batto was there sqatting at the corner of the verandah and looked at the roadside.

"All of them are like that. They come up with various promises. But after they get elected to the council they forget all their promises," another one who was at the courtyard said.

"Don't talk like that. Not all are like that," the man who was in the verandah said.

"Now, what if the Nilwala project materialises? How much we will benefit. This constant flooding will stop. We will be able to sow our paddy lands. Isn't it something extraordinary? That is not a small thing," said another.

"If such things work out like that, it's good. But what we say is that such things never happen. Now these council members have been elected to the council for many years. But none of them have been helpful for any project to stop flood here," the first man said again.

When heat of the election battle increased, Mahagedara *Ralahami* supported Dosthara Hamu and Podi Mahattaya supported Goring Hamu.

They held meetings all around the village and made innumerable promises. Everyone said that they were going to solve issues in the village. But none believed in their false promises.

"If someone asks to which party we would support, tell them that we are going to support both factions and don't mention that we are going to support one party," said Batto to all at home one evening.

"Yes, when they ask for our support, say yes to all. We can vote whoever we want," replied Addin in reply to his father.

Batto heard a new story that evening when he was at Podi Mahattaya's boutique.

"There's going to be a new bus service for the village it seems," said one who was sitting on the bench at the boutique to hear everyone there.

"A bus?" Do you know what had happened to it last time?" asked another in a strange tone.

"Why? What happened? They say the new bus will start operating from the first of next month," said the first man again.

"They have cancelled the idea of a bus, it seems," answered the other man.

"Why is that?"

"The reason is the power struggle, you know. Dosthara Hamu has been working hard to get the bus and finally has got the consent from the depot for the bus and they have been planning to start operations from the first of next month. But Goring Hamu has got to know about that and has met the minister and informed him that they would have to bear a loss, if the bus starts to operate. Then they cancelled the bus."

"Oh! What a loss!" said another youngster who was sitting on the bench. "It's loss on the part of the poor villagers; those who create obstructions for such decisions never travel in buses, they have cars."

"Hmm…, that's how things happen," said Batto getting up from the corner of the verandah to go home.

The election spree was high in the Athuraliya village with two to three days to go before the election. By that time about four to five election campaign groups had visited Batto's place as well as other houses in the village. Though only a few candidates were contesting for the election, many in the village had got themselves into groups and started their campaign by pleading for votes from villagers going door to door. Those who dared to step into Batto's house on other days were also bold enough to come and sit on the two old beds which were kept in the verandah.

There were a number of election offices established all over the village which belonged to the main parties contesting and their supporters were always present in those offices.

That day in the morning news spread across the village that the election battle had reached its height.

The party office belonging to Dosthara Hamu had been set on fire the previous night. Suspicion was directed towards Podi Mahattaya. There were only two days left for the election. Fire, people of the village thought was a bad omen of a series of events that were to occur in the village.

The same day evening, a group of people returning from a political meeting of Dosthara Hamu had been stoned. The culprits had been Podi Mahattaya's affiliates. That evening, police had been patrolling around the village and had taken two of his supporters into custody. But, Podi Mahattaya has been able to get them released within a few hours.

The next day, the situation deteriorated. That evening, Peter was coming towards Batto's house running. He was Podi Mahattaya's assistant in his boutique. Batto was squatting and removing some grass in his courtyard. Redi Nenda was inside the house. Babi was in the kitchen with her child. Addin was not at home.

"Batto Mame! Samy has been injured and taken to the hospital," said Podi Mahattaya's assistant who came running, breathing with difficulty.

"What? Why is that?" asked Batto.

Redi Nenda also came out of the kitchen hearing his noise.

"There had been a huge clash over there and many have got injured it seems. Samy has also been stabbed and his condition is quite bad," he continued.

"Oh, my lad!" Redi Nenda started to lament. Peter, the Podi Mahattaya's assistant ran back.

"These things are not done by anyone else but by himself" said Batto to his wife. She was sobbing.

"Why don't you go find some details. At least go see him tomorrow morning," pleaded Redi Nenda to Batto.

The fight had occurred between Podi Mahattaya's supporters and Mahagedara *Ralahami's*. Supporters from both parties had got injured. About seven or eight injured were taken to the hospital. Samy has been stabbed on his shoulder and therefore his condition was not serious.

Voting was to take place the following day. Addin also returned home when it was dark and by that time he also knew what had happened.

"It was all because of Samy Ayya's fault," said Addin to everyone at home. Redi Nenda was leaning against the door frame facing the courtyard, without talking but sobbing instead. As usually Batto was sitting on the string bed. Addin was sitting on the other bed at the other corner of the verandah.

"That's how things happen; our people are used as guinea pigs."

"It's another who gets elected to the council, while some others here fight with one another," said Addin with utmost sadness.

"Now, now, you may stop all these nonsensical stories. If one gets to know of what we discuss here, our lives too will be in danger," said Batto just like he recalled something.

"Did you hear any noise from the side of stile?" said Redi Nenda directing her head towards the stile. Batto and Addin too turned their heads towards the stile. It was pitch dark.

They heard the sound of a bicycle stopping at the stile. They saw someone coming towards the house crossing the stile in dark.

"Batto!" the person who came in the darkness called out to Batto.

He identified the person from his very voice.

"Oh, it's you, Podi Mahattaya! How is Samy now?" While asking Batto got up from the bed and walked forward. Redi Nenda and Addin also walked to the courtyard. Babi, also hearing his noise, came to the door and leaned on the door frame. Her son was also with her hanging on to her dress. Podi Mahattaya spoke to them.

"Samy's condition is not that serious. I am on my way back from the hospital. I looked into everything there. Goring Hamu will look after everything. More than our people, supporters from the otherside have got more injuries," said Podi Mahattaya.

Batto and others were listening to him with no reaction.

"Should I go see him at least tomorrow morning," Redi Nenda broke the silence.

"That's ok. I was, in fact, planning to come here some time early. Now, the main task is due tomorrow. Do not forget to caste your four votes. Hope you know Gorin Hamu's election symbol. I never came this way before as I trusted in you people. Don't worry about Samy's vote. We will take care of his vote. You may caste all your four votes early morning and get ready to leave for Matara," said Podi Mahattaya and handed a ten rupee note to Batto and left.

"These people would promise of so many things. But at last we would only get what Samy got at the end. I will not vote for anybody," said Redi Nenda after Podi Mahattaya left. She was suffering from what had happened to Samy.

"You may stop your nonsensical talks. After all, can we go against Podi Mahattaya's word. If we do so, it would be difficult for us to survive here," Batto said. "Do you think we could exist if Podi Mahattaya is angry with us other than anyone else."

"Whatever it is, if Goring Hamu wins, that would benefit Podi Mahattaya immensely," said Addin after a long pause.

"Hush! Hush! You may not open your mouth about this anymore," Batto said to Addin seriously.

"What a plight! People are not even allowed to vote freely according to their choice," said Addin again.

"It is none of your business. All of you should go and vote for Goring Hamu," said Batto sternly for everyone to hear.

24

"I should find some manual labour at least to feed this young one," said Babi one night. Batto and Addin were taking a rest in the verandah after serving themselves with boiled jack fruit, scraped coconut and *Lunu Miris* for dinner. They were not asleep. Babi put some jack fruit, *Lunu Miris* and scraped coconut into a clay bowl and placed it in her mother's hand. She served the remaining jackfruit into another bowl, sat on the coconut scraper and started to eat. Light of the bottle lamp fell on their faces.

"Where do you have manual labour? You be here consuming what we are providing," said Redi Nenda to Babi.

"How can I stay here forever. I should find something to feed my little one," Babi replied.

"Let him stay here. When he's big, he will help us in our work. Feeding him is not a big thing for us," said Redi Nenda to Babi.

Redi Nenda finished her food, washed the clay bowl from the water in the pot and walked to the verandah. Babi finished eating and started to clean up the kitchen. She swept the kitchen with an *ekel* broom and threw the garbage into the garbage pit. She closed the kitchen door and went inside the house with the bottle lamp in her hand.

When she came inside the house, she heard that everyone was talking about her.

"This is a period even Addin finds it difficult to find some work. How can she find work?" Babi could make out that it was Batto's voice.

"Ah! There is some work for *Akka*. I remembered only just now," Addin suggested.

"What is it?" asked Redi Nenda stepping out of the house to the verandah. At the same time Babi came to the door and leaned on its frame.

"Podi Mahattaya is building a new boat to collect sand from the river. If we ask him, *Akka* also might be able a get some work there." With that news everyone was hopeful. "I too was wondering whether I would be able to get some work there. Anyway, it would require about seven to eight people."

"I too heard people talking about it at the boutique. They were talking that it might take at least another one month to finish its work," said Batto reminiscing what he had heard.

"Why don't you speak to Samy, about this," suggested Redi Nenda.

Podi Mahattaya was in the process of making a boat. Three or four carpenters were working on it. There were already three-four locations where river sand was mined and people from Matara and its vicinity used to come there to buy sand. Podi Mahattaya's boat was the first in the village to venture into this business in a mass scale.

Both Addin and Babi got to work in Podi Mahattaya's boat as sand collectors.

Addin left for work early morning and got on to the boat along with others and sailed it up to a point until they found sand. Four others went with him on the boat. Addin found it quite fun to ride the boat upstream and downstream on the river. They used to stop the boat at a place where there was sand. Then others took cane baskets and dove in the river and brought back baskets full of sand and filled the boat with it. They had to fill the whole boat with sand. It used to take a long time to dive continuously and fill the boat with sand. Sand mining was a very difficult task. The work started in the morning and went on till about ten o'clock. It was difficult to continue to do it any longer. Therefore, they were only able to make about two boats of sand in one day. It was not easy to be in deep water and bring sand up for long.

They were paid according to the number of boatful of sands they brought ashore which was divided among the five of them.

They used to bring the boat filled with sand ashore and tie it to a tree. Then it was ready to unload the sand in the boat to the shore.

There were four to five women to unload the sand at the river bank. Babi was also among them. She went to the ferry with her kid. Two in the boat used to fill their baskets with sand and then she and others got those on their heads and emptied them onto a pile of sand.

They were being paid by Podi Mahattaya and she used to take that money and go with her kid to the boutique close-by. She used to take her breakfast with her kid and it became a custom for them everyday. Then she returned home by noon and started to prepare lunch for her parents who were slapping clothes on the stone and washing at the river. In the afternoon she used to help her mother and father with their work.

Babi liked this job as she was able to earn something daily. She only wanted a meager amount for the survival of her kid and herself. She could fulfil that requirement from this new job and therefore she liked to go there to work in the boat.

But, Addin was into this as he had no other work to do. Addin went for manual labour too whenever he got the opportunity if that paid him well.

It was easy to bring sand ashore during the dry season, but it became more arduous when it rained. It was difficult for them to work on days when the water level in the river went up after heavy rains. Therefore, the actual number of days they could work were limited. Though Podi Mahattaya was able to earn some extra bucks by selling sand at a higher price during such rainy periods, Babi and Addin were unable to earn a penny as they couldn't work on rainy days.

25

One day a car stopped on the tar road in front of Batto's house. One young person got down from the car came forward and stopped in front of the stile and looked inquisitively towards Batto's house. He was in a black trouser and a white shirt. There was another inside the car.

Babi heard the sound of the car. Her kid was playing outside the house. Neither Batto nor Redi Nenda were around to be seen.

The kid seeing the vehicle stationed on the road, ran into the house and stopped near Babi.

"Why *Putha*?" she peeped through the door.

She saw the car at the stile and instead of greeting the visitors; she ran to the back of the house and called her mother.

"*Ammaa!*"

"Why? Why the hell are you shouting?"

"Someone has come," shouted and replied Babi.

Redi Nenda came towards the house hurriedly and went towards the tar road. The visitor was still at the stile on the roadside. She could not recognise the visitor. The motor car was still on the road, stationed.

"Who are you searching for, sir?" Redi Nenda asked while reaching the stile.

"Is there one called Addin here?" asked the visitor.

"Yes, but why sir?" asked Redi Nenda suspiciously. Babi was at the verandah looking at them. Her son was hanging on to her dress.

"Can I meet, Addin?" asked the visitor.

"Why sir? Where are you from?" Redi Nenda was still feeling suspicious.

"I have come from Matara. I want to meet Addin," said the young visitor.

"Addin may have gone somewhere. But he will be here soon," replied Redi Nenda looking towards the road.

"Oh! There he comes! Just as I mentioned," Redi Nenda said looking at the road again.

The visitor turned towards the road.

"When I went to the boutique, the people told me that someone has come to see me. That's why I came here quickly," said Addin and walked towards the visitor. Redi Nenda was still on the other side of the stile looking at them.

"Who are you, sir?"

"Can't you recognise me, Addin?" asked the visitor smiling at Addin.

"No, I can't recognise you," said Addin looking at the visitor suspiciously.

"Do you remember that you used to work in a boutique in Matara sometime ago?" asked the visitor.

"Yes, then?"

"Do you remember the owner of that boutique?"

"Oh! You are his son is'nt it?"

"Yes, I am," said the visitor smiling.

"Oh! How could I recognise you? You were a small child at that time, now you're big," said Addin.

"Come inside the house, sir. This's my mother," said Addin again.

"No, this is fine. We've got to go soon."

"So. How are you, sir? It has been a long time. How's your father doing now?"

"My father passed away three years ago. I am the one who takes care of his business now."

"So, what made you come this way, sir?" asked Addin.

"My father had told me about you several times when he was alive. If I am to take someone to work in the shop, he told me to take you somehow. My father had high esteem for your work. I opened up a new hotel recently. We need people to work there and they have to be trustworthy too. So I remembered you. I thought you would come join me. So I came here to take you with me."

Addin was listening what he said with a stupid smile.

"Now itself?" asked Addin.

"Yes Addin, it would be easy if you could come with us now. You can go in the car with us," replied the visitor looking at Addin as well as Redi Nenda.

"We need you only for a short period. A lot of government officers are coming to our hotel now. I can later get you a peon post in a government office. It is good for you and others in your family," the visitor said.

"*Amme*, shall I go?" Addin asked his mother who was still at the courtyard.

"There's no point in staying here either. You will be doing manual work here. Why not go if you would be able to get a peon post," replied Redi Nenda looking at the visitor.

Batto Vidane hastened his strides seeing a car in front of his house. He saw the young man outside the car and another one sitting in the car. He took the kerchief which was on his shoulder into his hand and smiled at the visitor obediently. He crossed the stile and stepped on to the courtyard.

By that time, Addin dressed in a shirt and a sarong, was almost ready to go with the visitor. Redi Nenda was with him. Babi was leaning on the door frame of the house looking at them. Her son was still hanging on to her dress.

"We were waiting for you. Where have you been for all this time?" Redi Nenda got the lead to ask Batto.

"Why?" Batto asked innocently.

"That sir, here, is the son of the Mudalali where Addin was working in Matara. He has come here to take Addin with him. He would be given a job in his new hotel it seems. Later, he says he could arrange him a peon post in a government office," Redi Nenda explained the situation to him.

"Yes, *Appochchi*. I am going with him. I have been unable to find work here nowadays," said Addin.

"If that's good for you, do I care?" said Batto in a bored tone. The visiting young man placed a ten rupee note in Batto's hand.

Batto and the others thought it was such a grace for the owner of the hotel to come here to take Addin in his own car.

"What an honor if he is able to find a peon job in a government office. He is such a nice gentleman," said Redi Nenda after Addin left. Therefore, all of them started to dwell in a new hope. It was as if fortune came in search of Addin, they thought.

Batto went to the ferry of the river early morning with Redi Nenda and washed clothes. Babi went to work for sand mining in the morning and returned home by noon. Samy became a partner in Podi Mahattaya's *Kasippu* business. He did not do anything for his family. Redi Nenda distributed the cleaned clothes to houses in the evening. This was the routine of the Batto family. Redi Nenda and Babi were of the view that Addin would one day be able to resurrect the whole family from this misery. But, Batto never believed totally in it. Therefore, he was always of the view that they should not be so hopeful. If Redi Nenda or Babi said something, Batto opposed them.

"It is bad to keep unnecessary hopes on anything," Batto said on such occasions.

One day Addin returned home about six months after he left home. Redi Nenda and Babi were happy and impatient to know about his new job. But something had happened different from what they expected.

"I will never go there again," said Addin firmly.

"Why is that?" asked Redi Nenda.

"It's such a burden. Even though he promised me so many things, I was ill-treated. I had to work from early morning till about eleven o'clock in the night. I couldn't even take rest for a minute. I wanted to come home twice. But he never allowed me to come. Mudalali's son is worse than the dead father. He never cared for our salary and food. We had to work like slaves," Addin explained everything.

"What happened to the peon post he promised?" asked Babi disturbing his talk.

"I asked about it twice. It was an effort in vain. Whenever I inquired about it, he said he would look into it later. So, I thought this was not going to do any good to me. Not only me, others who worked there were also not paid well. But we had to work like slaves. So, I asked for permission to go home about twice. But he never allowed. At last I decided to come home. He only fooled us."

"Oh! In vain!" Cursed Babi to the Mudalali.

Redi Nenda blamed Mudalali. There was nothing they could do other than blame him.

Batto was listening to the utterances of Addin, Redi Nenda and Babi patiently.

They had something to eat for dinner that day and were talking endlessly at the verandah. But, Batto remained silent. He was listening to others lying on his string bed. At the end of the conversation, he got up from the bed, sat on it and joined the conversation.

"Addin! None of them suit us. It's no point blaming others. Whatever it may be, only one job suits us. That's this washing job. We have been doing it for generations. We know how to do it properly, and only we know how to do it and no one else. So, don't run here and there searching for other jobs. You may do this washing job to the best. You will never go wrong if you do this properly. We only need some money to buy something to fill our tummies," said Batto to everyone and no one spoke against him. That comment was mainly aimed at Addin.

"But, how can that be so? Are we going to commit our lives for this job? Are we going to depend everything on the *Wellawa* forever? We also should have a right to live just as others. We wash clothes as we have nothing else to do." Addin had never spoken so rudely in his life and he felt sad about the attitude of his father. He was looking at Batto in the semi-darkness. He thought his father was looking very old and that time had come to give up his job and hand over everything for the next generation. He felt deep sympathy on his father's life.

"You may stop all this talking now and go to sleep," said Redi Nenda to Addin.

Batto thought that Addin had changed a lot during this little period. Now he was a matured young man.

It was after so many months that Addin was able sleep on his bed at the verandah. But sleep never came to him for a long time. He was in pensive mood for hours.

But he thought that he has determined to do one thing. His mind was aimed strongly at one single matter which was shown by his father. 'Reason for all these hardships is not considering the value of their labour of cleaning clothes of others by villagers who are thinking that we are a substandard category of people who belong to a low caste. They consider that the cleaning of clothes is a duty of our clan. He must come to a firm decision,' he thought. Thinking all this he fell asleep.

The next day Addin got up with a somewhat slothful mood. This time it was Addin who took the pile of clothes onto his shoulder instead of his mother and father. He stepped on to the courtyard to go to the ferry of the river. Babi, Redi Nenda and Batto were watching him going towards the river. His slothfulness never left him even until he went to the ferry of the river. His mind was full of new thoughts. He had the new ideas for a new approach of his own job. He had an understanding that no one could be defeated if he does it correctly and devotedly, even an unworthy thing. He could see a new light before him in the dawn when he arrived at the ferry of the river. 'I must get the real value of my labour of cleaning of clothes of others. This could be the path to a better life for our family,' he thought.

●●●

GLOSSARY

Akka – elder sister

Amma, Amme – mother.

Appochchi – father.

Arachchi – peon of the Government Agent.

Ataka naataka wepata sungam – an indoor game traditionally played by rural children.

Ayya – elder brother.

Disapathithuma – Government Agent.

Gramasewaka Ralahami – village headman.

Hamine – elderly woman in a family in rural areas

Hamine – mother in a rural family.

Hamu – person of some elite families of the village.

Jangiya – a simple dress having openings for head, two arms and two legs.

Kasippu – a type of an illicit liquor produced in rural areas.

Kasippu Wadiya – temporary place arranged for producing illicit liquor.

Kella – a girl.

Keum – traditional sort of rice cakes.

Kokis – traditional cookies.

Kotahalu magula – function taken when a girl attains puberty.

Kuruniya – traditional scale (bowl) used to measure paddy.

Lunu miris – hot and tasty dish prepared from chillis, Maldive fish and salt.

Malli – younger brother.

Mudalali – trader.

Nekath Mama – traditional astrologer in the village who also belongs to a low caste.

Pawada – clean white clothe laid before a procession of a wedding or a funeral to walk on. Purpose of this is to pay the respect to the wedding or the dead body.

Pawada – sometime ago in rural communities there was a custom of laying white cloth before the people to walk on, when an important function was taking place. Laying *Pawada* was the duty of the washing community in the village.

Punchi Ayya – younger boy of two elder brothers of a family.

Putha – son

Rada gedara – house of the washing community.

Radawa, Radav, Rada – person who belongs to the washing community. This term is generally used to disgrace a person.

Ralahami – former village headman.

Redi Nenda, Nenda, Nende – elderly women of the families of the washing community.

Vidane, Vidane Mama – elderly man of a family of washing community.

Weda mahattaya – indigenous doctor practicing in the village.

Wellawa, Wella heliya – traditional device used by the washing community to boil clothes in water vapours.

Weralu – a type of a small fruit.

Wiyana – in the earlier times when there was a function in a rural house they put up a celing-like shade under the roof using pieceso of clean white cloth.

STERLING

Recent Fiction Novel

Kalyug is the story of a young couple Raghav and Mandira who are busy enjoying themselves when a series of unfortunate events turn everything upside down for them. As the story progresses, the mystery deepens. This is an intriguing thriller which keeps you glued right from the first chapter until the end.

ISBN 978 93 86245 64 9   Price: ₹190
mail@sterlingpublishers.in
www.sterlingpublishers.in
Also available amazon.in

STERLING

Recent Fiction Novel

This compelling story about twins comes from a young teenager. It is a light, yet a gripping one about fraternal twins, Jaidev and Tara, a brother and a sister, and the inexplicable bond they share. It takes you through the alleys of their childhood memories, their life today, and the ups and downs a brother-sister relation goes through while growing years.

ISBN: 978 93 86245 43 4   Price: ₹190
mail@sterlingpublishers.in
www.sterlingpublishers.in
Also available amazon.in

STERLING

Recent Fiction Novel

We see them everywhere and yet make them invisible. We don't tell their stories because we can't identify with them. The Street is that untold story about the life of the people, who live and grow on the street. Surrounded with various threats, yet how they make space for the thrills of life is all that you get to experience in the book. It explores the daily struggle for survival of street children and the freedom they cherish and aspire.

ISBN: 978 93 86245 40 3   Price: ₹350
mail@sterlingpublishers.in
www.sterlingpublishers.in
Also available amazon.in